MW00463355

TWELVE DRUMMERS DRUMMING

Twelve Days of Christmas

Emily E K Murdoch

© Copyright 2022 by Emily E K Murdoch
Text by Emily E K Murdoch
Cover by Dar Albert

Dragonblade Publishing, Inc. is an imprint of Kathryn Le Veque Novels, Inc.
P.O. Box 23
Moreno Valley, CA 92556
ceo@dragonbladepublishing.com

Produced in the United States of America

First Edition September 2022
Trade Paperback Edition

Reproduction of any kind except where it pertains to short quotes in relation to advertising or promotion is strictly prohibited.

All Rights Reserved.

The characters and events portrayed in this book are fictitious. Any similarity to real persons, living or dead, is purely coincidental and not intended by the author.

ARE YOU SIGNED UP FOR DRAGONBLADE'S BLOG?

You'll get the latest news and information on exclusive giveaways, exclusive excerpts, coming releases, sales, free books, cover reveals and more.

Check out our complete list of authors, too!

No spam, no junk. That's a promise!

Sign Up Here

www.dragonbladepublishing.com

Dearest Reader;

Thank you for your support of a small press. At Dragonblade Publishing, we strive to bring you the highest quality Historical Romance from some of the best authors in the business. Without your support, there is no 'us', so we sincerely hope you adore these stories and find some new favorite authors along the way.

Happy Reading!

CEO, Dragonblade Publishing

Additional Dragonblade books by Author Emily E K Murdoch

Twelve Days of Christmas
Twelve Drummers Drumming
Eleven Pipers Piping
Ten Lords a Leaping
Nine Ladies Dancing

The De Petras Saga
The Misplaced Husband (Book 1)
The Impoverished Dowry (Book 2)
The Contrary Debutante (Book 3)
The Determined Mistress (Book 4)
The Convenient Engagement (Book 5)

The Governess Bureau Series
A Governess of Great Talents (Book 1)
A Governess of Discretion (Book 2)
A Governess of Many Languages (Book 3)
A Governess of Prodigious Skill (Book 4)
A Governess of Unusual Experience (Book 5)
A Governess of Wise Years (Book 6)
A Governess of No Fear (Novella)

Never The Bride Series
Always the Bridesmaid (Book 1)
Always the Chaperone (Book 2)
Always the Courtesan (Book 3)
Always the Best Friend (Book 4)
Always the Wallflower (Book 5)
Always the Bluestocking (Book 6)
Always the Rival (Book 7)
Always the Matchmaker (Book 8)

The Lyon's Den Connected World

Pirates of Britannia Series

De Wolfe Pack: The Series

Dear reader,

I adore Christmas, and I've chosen to include a few Christmas traditions in this story that embellishes the timeline. Though I haven't kept 100% to the historical record, I've chosen to do this to surround you with yuletide galore, so you can fall in love with my heroes and heroines in a glorious Christmas setting,

Enjoy!
Emily x

CHAPTER ONE

"AND SO, WE would like to announce," the young man said, his hair flying wildly around his face as he looked excitedly out at the family gathered in the room, "that we are engaged to be married!"

Cheers and sighs erupted all around the room as Dr. Stuart Walsingham looked at Caroline Forrest with adoring eyes.

Women in empire-line dresses moved forward to clasp Caroline's hands in theirs, and Stuart was clapped on the back by his future father-in-law. All was merriment and laughter, joy and celebration.

There was, however, one person in the room not taken with this news.

Jemima Fitzroy smiled thinly, her lips pressed together in the only expression she could manage. She would not offend, not if she could help it. Her father wished them all to be a family, and she would not disappoint him for the world.

Probably.

As women cooed over the couple—the first of the family to become betrothed—Jemima watched from her seat by the window. It was like looking into another world, another family.

Not her own.

"The first Fitzroy wedding!" her father was exclaiming. "Goodness me, I shall have to hope you do not all wish to marry in the same Season, or I shall be ruined!"

Laughter echoed around the room. Jemima did not join them.

Well, he was not wrong, she thought irritably. Her father certainly had enough daughters.

As the eldest, and the only daughter of his first wife, Jemima considered herself her father's keeper. She had not been amused when he had married Selina, a widow who came with two daughters of her own.

Caroline and Esther were all very well, as stepsisters went. Jemima had to admit that as their parents had married so many years ago, she could hardly remember her own mother.

But of course, it had not stayed three sisters for long. Her father and Selina had produced three more daughters, Arabella, Lucy, and Sophia.

More Fitzroys than the world knew what to do with, and that didn't include their cousins…

Jemima pursed her lips as wisps of conversation floated around the drawing room.

"—such a handsome man—"

"—all saw it coming, of course—"

"—married by Michaelmas, if I have my way—"

Though her stepsister's engagement was not a cause for celebration in her mind, as she looked around the room, she could see she was alone in that regard.

Jemima swallowed, but the words she attempted to swallow down poured from her mouth. "I wish you had not interrupted my talk with Father—I have been hoping to speak to him about the war for some time now. Hundreds of people, not just I, have signed it to support our soldiers in the continuing war in France, yet—"

Caroline's eyes were bright with the excitement of all the attention, but she still managed to roll her eyes. "Again, Jemima? We have listened to this time and time again, and still, you will not quit your obsession with this war!"

"With peace!" Jemima spoke fervently, her hands clasped in her lap and her heart starting to patter with the passion of her words. "For it is peace I strive for and many others across the country! Why should the depths of human depravity be permitted to continue when so many are suffering? Why do we not support our men as they return, leaving them to suffer on the streets?"

Her half-sister Arabella smiled patiently, but there was no interest in her expression. "Jemima, please…"

"As long as I can remember, we have been at war with France!" Jemima spoke, certain she would one day help her sisters to understand. "Yet I am sure the people of France have no such wish to be at war at all! If only we, the people of Britain, could come together and—"

But her family wasn't listening. They did not understand, not really.

They suffered, she knew, and she wished for that suffering to end. Could not the world live in peace, rather than continuously fight wars over lines on a map?

Her stepmother, Selina, was occupied with preventing tears from falling and bemoaning that not all her daughters were present to witness such a day.

"It is simply too bad poor Esther and Lucy departed not one day before this happy time," Selina spoke petulantly. "They would decide to go to Bath, and determined as they were to enjoy all the fashionable treats of the coming Christmas season, they will be with their cousins Joy and Harmony now, though I cannot think the Bath Fitzroys will have news as festive as this!"

Jemima was not so sure about that. Though Esther and Lucy were certainly not flirts, a terrible accusation for any young lady, heads would turn to follow those flame-colored tresses now they had been let loose in Bath society.

She alone had the coloring of her father, a light brown, seemingly washed out amongst the dazzling sight of her sisters.

Now they were a household of six daughters—something

their father had failed to consider at the time of their births—it was all too easy to become lost in the noise.

It had mattered little when they were children. There was always someone shouting, someone who had scraped a knee, someone who was sobbing over their embroidery.

Now they were young ladies and had scandalized Society by permitting Caroline, Jemima, Arabella, and Esther to all be out together.

Gentlemen at clubs had shaken their heads, and ladies had tutted at Almack's. At least, that was what Jemima had heard.

With so many ladies at home, the gossip was that Arthur Fitzroy was unable to keep his women in order...

Jemima's eyes flickered around the room. The November evening was dark, but there were red candles with gold ribbons around them affixed all around the room where the family had gathered.

Advent Sunday, the day Christmas excitement truly began.

Holly and ivy had been placed around the room by Mrs. Castle, their housekeeper, ready for the festive season. Wreaths of the same were adorning all doors in their London home, and there was even a bunch of mistletoe hanging in the hallway for unsuspecting visitors, something Jemima certainly did not approve of.

Her father was still talking to the happy couple. "Oh, Walsingham, such wonderful news! Tell me, how precisely..."

Jemima sighed at she looked at them all. After waiting all day for his attention, she had only just started to speak with her father when the family had trooped in, led by Caroline, who apparently had news to share. Now the moment had passed.

Dr. Stuart Walsingham had seemingly forgotten to release her stepsister. She was clasped to his side, a gaggle of her sisters gathered around her.

"Oh, Caroline," breathed Sophia, "it is too much to believe! You and Dr. Walsingham—engaged! Indeed, I cannot believe it!"

Sophia was the youngest of the family at only thirteen, and

her wide eyes confirmed her disbelief. She, too, had the red hair that all of Selina's children had inherited, and as Jemima looked around the room, the candlelight illuminated her sisters Caroline and Sophia until their hair gleamed burgundy.

Caroline beamed at Sophia and held out her left hand. On her finger sat a gold band with a large diamond, throwing sparkles of light around the room.

"My word," Sophia said, reaching out and tilting her sister's hand so the diamond glittered, "Dr. Walsingham has bought you an engagement ring! Only the very finest people are doing so you know, 'tis the height of fashion."

Circles of light were flashing around the room as Caroline's engagement ring sparkled, and Jemima blinked as it shone into her eyes.

When her vision returned, her gaze fell on her stepmother, blinking back tears. Caroline had always been Selina's favorite. She appeared almost overcome with joy and pride as she gazed at her daughter.

Caroline had only laughter as her reply to the cries of joy from her family. Her face shone with happiness, and she turned her head to smile at the man she had promised to spend the rest of her life with.

On the other side of the room, nearer where Jemima was sitting, sat Arabella. Just a few years shy of Jemima's twenty-one, Arabella had been present at almost all of the occasions when Caroline and Dr. Walsingham had met. Her discussion with her father was on the wedding and exactly who should be invited.

"The Coleridges, of course," Arabella said seriously. Her face was generally serious, Jemima reminded herself, and it was not necessarily a sign of disapproval. However much Jemima might wish it. "And the Halls, we must not forget them."

"I do not believe that we shall have the final say, you know," said Sophia slowly with a smile from across the room. Sophia had a love of teasing and found Arabella a frequently unwitting victim. "Perhaps we shall have to ensure all the blacksmiths in town are in attendance, or station a large bear near the altar."

Arabella stared wide-eyed at her sister until the laughter of Sophia and their father told her that she was once again subject to her sister's ridicule. Ruffled, but unsurprised at her sister's teasing, she smoothed down her gown and averted her gaze from her family's laughter. Standing slowly, she moved over to sit beside Jemima.

"It is such a wonderful piece of news, is it not?" Arabella said gently.

Jemima smiled. "I know our parents are certainly pleased. I just wish that I could have brought them such happiness."

"Fie, Jemima," scolded Arabella softly as the rest of their family continued their laughter. "You know Papa is immensely proud of you, for many reasons."

"Name one," Jemima said dully. "Name just one, and I shall be satisfied. He is so ashamed of my pacifism that he has tried to make me promise not to attend any rallies!"

Arabella opened her mouth, hesitated, then closed it. She looked at her half-sister pityingly, something Jemima loathed. But what could she say? How to explain to her sisters just how...how alone she felt in this crowd?

"Do not ask me to name a particular time, or a particular place, that his pride in you has been demonstrated," Arabella said quietly under the general hubbub of the room. "You know my memory does not serve me as well as yours, and I am sure—"

"It is as I thought," said Jemima. She breathed out slowly and pasted a smile onto her face. "Do not fret about me, Arabella," she said softly. "I truly am happy for Caroline, especially as Dr. Walsingham seems to be such a gentle and kind young man."

Arabella looked at her sister shrewdly. "You cannot hide your true feelings from us, you know."

"I know." Jemima tried to rearrange her face so that the smile she had put there looked more genuine. "But I can from him. Walsingham. I have no wish to offend Caroline's beau."

Arabella shook her head with a smile. "Ever since I can remember, you have not been one for hiding your emotions!" Her smile became more serious. "I do not think that you need to marry in order to please Papa."

Jemima shook her head. "Then why does he speak of it so often, and so forcefully? Why does he always insist on accompanying me to any occasion which I have been invited to, encouraging me to speak to every young man in attendance?"

It was mortifying. Jemima shivered at just one recollection of their attendance at the Halls' only last week. His insistence that she dance with every gentleman there—it was scandalous!

She would gain a reputation if he were not careful.

"I truly believe he only wants you to find a husband."

"And what if I do not want a husband?" Jemima challenged, keeping her voice low in a whisper so no one, save Arabella, could hear her.

Arabella blinked. She was the one sister Jemima ever confided in, but that did not mean Arabella often understood her elder sister. "Not…not want a husband?"

Jemima sighed and placed her hand gently on that of her sister's as words failed her.

Was she the only Fitzroy, she wondered, that looked beyond marriage and looked at the world? Looked at the fighting that had torn France asunder—did no one mark the mentions of the dead in the newspapers?

"Forget my words, they were ill-spoken," she said quietly. "As the eldest child of our Father and your mother, you are the most comfortable in this family, and you are our natural peacemaker."

Though it was more, Jemima thought. Arabella's serious temperament, paired with her genuine love of her sisters, almost always placed her in the center of sisterly trouble.

"Perhaps. You have not smiled truly since the announcement," Arabella said in an undertone.

Jemima swallowed. Blast Arabella and her careful notice of others. Though welcome at times, this was not one of them. "Caroline and I are the same age, almost to the day. I am but a month older, and this closeness has forced an unspoken competitiveness that she cannot help but crow over me!"

"You allow yourself to be driven to irritation on almost a daily basis," returned Arabella, softly. "It is not Caroline's fault she is more frequently invited to card parties, or to dinner—nor if she is more frequently missed if unable to attend."

"Yet in her first week, she elicited the smiles and compliments I did not in my first Season."

At the age of one and twenty, Jemima had suffered through five Seasons.

Most of her peers, those who had stepped out into Society in 1808, were carrying their second child for the men they had been encouraged to marry, yet she had not even received one offer.

Even Esther, who was nineteen, and Lucy who was a mere sixteen, had attracted more attention than she had.

Now Caroline was to be married.

Arabella's eyes flickered over to the other side of the room and saw Caroline laugh, throwing back her head so her long neck gracefully tilted. "In Caroline's defense, she seems unaware of comparisons, regardless of who makes them, between you two. She has never striven to better you. I have heard her on more than one occasion encourage young men of her acquaintance to talk with you, dance with you, spend time with—"

Another laugh from Caroline muffled Arabella's voice, and Jemima laughed darkly. "Oh yes, completely unaware."

Where did it come from, this petty jealousy? Jemima hated it, hated herself for seeing it. But always being compared: not as pretty as Caroline, not as witty as Caroline, not as charming as Caroline…

Sophia was jesting with their father about the different wedding clothes their sister was to buy for her trousseau.

"And a fisherman's smock, obviously," said their father in a deep serious tone, Sophia in fits of giggle beside her. "Where will our Caroline be without her ability to catch trout?"

Despite herself, despite her absolute denial to her father that she should marry at all, Jemima flushed with shame.

Within a year or two, she would be considered too old to marry at all, and her chances of finding anyone would have disappeared.

It was not that she was without beauty or elegance or character or even wealth! She knew her dowry from her mother was substantial. Six thousand pounds was not a sum of money to be sniffed at.

She certainly possessed many of the necessary features to be considered beautiful. Her light brown hair curled naturally, and she was slightly taller than all of her sisters. Her lean frame could have done with slightly more padding in certain areas, but the empire-line dresses complemented her figure. And her eyes, shining as they were, were certainly pleasing.

Jemima knew all this. She had a looking glass and saw the woman blink back at her each evening before she was trotted out to meet yet more people.

A wry smile appeared across her lips. Her real trouble, not that she would ever admit it to anyone, that she had encountered in each of the five Seasons she had been paraded around by her father and Selina, was that she was no one's fool.

Forceful when she thought she was right, blunt when she couldn't help but be honest, most people found her…what was it Selina had said?

"A difficult conversation partner at the best of times."

Jemima sighed as she looked at her sisters, all charming, all elegant. As each year passed without any invitations to courtship, her father and stepmother would exchange concerned glances.

Yet Caroline…

"That is the reason, after all," Jemima said bitterly, "that this celebration is so effusive, you must admit. At the same age as I, we all feared—unspoken, of course—that Caroline had also missed her chance of matrimony. Yet, here is Stuart Walsingham, determined to marry her and make the entire Fitzroy family practically giddy with joy."

Jemima felt sick. *These thoughts are getting you nowhere,* she scolded herself. *Ignore them and pay attention to the moment at hand. Try to be happy for her.*

"Jemima!" Arabella was shocked—and, Jemima thought, rightly so. "You must be tired. Come, let us join the family."

Bracing herself, Jemima turned her eyes and ears to the rest of the room's inhabitants, but almost immediately regretted doing so when she realized her stepmother was speaking.

"...finest day of a mother's life," she was saying, tears blossoming in her eyes as she spoke, "to see her daughter find someone who can make her as happy—nay, happier—than her parents. And now this day has come for our eldest child."

Arthur drew a loving arm around his wife, and the two of them beamed at Caroline.

And that was the moment Jemima lost her temper.

"Excuse me!" she said loudly, rising from her chair with her arms crossed so tightly they may have been stitched there.

The entirety of the room turned, and Jemima could instantly tell from their confused and rather startled faces they had completely forgotten that she had been sitting there.

Jemima smiled thinly. "I hate to point this out, but *I* am actually the eldest child."

Selina's mouth fell slightly open, and Jemima's suspicions were confirmed. Were there daughters who truly loved their stepmothers? She had tried to love Selina, tried with all her might, but Selina had always loved her daughters so much more.

Jemima had ignored it as a child. She had not permitted it to injure her when she had first been announced to Society.

But no more.

"What you meant to say," Jemima continued, her voice low and steady. She was not going to lose her temper...she was determined not to lose her temper, "was that Caroline is *your* eldest child. Papa's eldest child is me."

"Well, of course!" Selina swallowed, suddenly looking nervous. "You know that is what I meant—"

"Then why didn't you say it?" said Jemima, her voice carrying all the hurt which had been brewing for the last ten minutes. "Papa, I had really wished to speak to you, do you have any time now?"

Arthur looked around the room hesitantly. "Naturally, my dear, I will stay a while with Caroline and Dr. Walsingham as—"

"I see," Jemima said bitterly. The pain she felt was surely written across her face; she had never been very good at hiding her emotions. "I see now that only if I can bring a gentleman to this house will I be listened to. The fact that thousands of men have perished while we sit here and chatter about how many roses Caroline must have is of no importance. No matter. I shall see myself out."

Jemima strode to the door, ignoring the calls from both her father and a few of her sisters to stay. She regretted it immediately, of course. It was always the way with her furious temper, but there was nothing for it.

She had nothing to say to Caroline and Dr. Walsingham, and no words could prevent her from storming out of the room and of their home.

CHAPTER TWO

THE FURY, THE anger, the hurt coursing through Jemima's veins gave her the strength to battle through the winter cold, and she almost forgot she had left her entire family behind. Caroline was probably upset she had gone.

But Jemima did not think about that, could not think about that. As she pushed past a gaggle of people, she almost fell to the ground as she tripped over a stone in the road as she crossed the street.

There was always somewhere to storm off to when you lived in London. Unfortunately, what Jemima could not find at this present moment was peace of mind.

All she wanted to do was walk without giving any thought as to where she was going, fury and embarrassment burning through her lungs.

She would have to go back at some point. Have to face them.

"Jemima!" A voice cried out behind her, and Jemima closed her eyes in frustration.

Was she ever to be left alone? Was the hunt for a husband never to end, were the comments on her ability to "catch" a man never to cease? When would someone take her interests seriously?

She turned and looked into her sister Arabella's serious eyes. "You were truly going to leave without even a pelisse?"

Arabella appeared to have grabbed one at random, a long luxurious pelisse lined with fur. One glance told Jemima it was Esther's, but that seemed rather beside the point.

"I am not cold, you may take the pelisse back with you."

All she could hear in her head were the words of her stepmother: *now this day has come for our eldest child.*

Tears threatened to escape from her eyes, but she dashed them away. She would not cry on Selina's account. She refused to.

Arabella looked at her suspiciously as Jemima shivered, her crimson gown whipped by the chilling wind. "Jemima. You must not mind Mama. You know she does not speak out of malice."

"Then she does not think, so injures me doubly," Jemima could not help but let the sarcasm flow from her mind to her tongue. She reached out her hand to pull her gown in from the teasing wind. "The very fact this is a common occurrence merely proves her inability to consider my feelings, time after time after—"

"It is difficult for her," Arabella interrupted. They were almost separated as two street urchins ran between them. "You know that she has tried to keep you at the center of our family."

"Well then, she has failed. I cannot help but say it, and it brings me no pleasure I assure you. The last thing I feel is the center of this family. Any family."

Before Arabella could reply, Jemima turned on her heels and strode off in the opposite direction.

It was not, Jemima reminded herself, that Selina was an unfair person in general. She did like her stepmother.

Selina was caring, thoughtful, and had always encouraged her daughters Caroline and Esther to befriend Jemima.

But Jemima was old enough now to understand the real problem. Selina found it difficult to love Jemima. The only child out of six who was not hers, Selina had tried desperately to treat them all the same but invariably failed.

"Steady on there, steady on!" A portly gentleman with a stick raised it at her angrily.

Jemima realized, lost in her thoughts as she was, that she had just walked straight into him.

"My apologies, sir," she said stiffly and walked away before she had to listen to his angry words.

Jemima reached the end of the street and paused.

Where was she? Gazing up at the street names, she saw she had been walking almost in a complete circle. She was very nearly home.

Jemima gazed out across the London street. There was never anywhere as busy as London, and she reveled in the hustle and bustle of it all.

Even here in the street there was just so much happening.

As they were now approaching December, the signs of the festive Christmas season were beginning to spring up everywhere she looked. Many of the shop fronts had ribbons of red and gold around their doors, and most had special notices of Christmas treats were available inside.

Across the way from her was a man standing on a box, shouting news from France.

"And the glorious war is almost over!" He shouted in a shrill voice, his suit and jacket splattered with mud as though he had stood there for hours. "Our brave men have fought valiantly, and as we welcome them home..."

Jemima turned to look further down the street where a small market had been erected and fruit and vegetables were being hawked.

"Get your potatoes here!" squawked a woman in a rather shabby overcoat. It had once been blue, Jemima could see, but it had been many years since it had been washed out to a dull grey. "Get your parsnips and radishes, keep the winter cold at bay!"

"Sweetmeats!" A man cried beside her, plying his own wares from a stall he pushed on wheels. "Hot, warm, juicy, get your sweetmeats!"

Children were playing up and down the street, and Jemima

immediately picked out those only pretending to play whilst they ruthlessly and mercilessly pickpocketed the respectable gentlemen walking up and down the street.

Hidden by the presence of children genuinely playing, only a true Londoner like Jemima would have been able to spot them. She saw one boy make off with what looked from a distance like a large gold pocket watch.

There were gaggles of women laughing, and a line of children led by a schoolmistress.

"Keep in line!" was the phrase she kept uttering without a backward glance. "Keep in line!"

Jemima was not entirely sure where, but somewhere close by was a choir.

"Good King Wenceslas looked out, on the feast of Stephen..."

The cacophony was almost overwhelming, but for Jemima it was welcome, shouting down her angry thoughts and restoring her calm.

There was nowhere like London to lose yourself. With all of the noise in the street, it was almost possible for her to forget how cold she was, how irritated she was with everything.

Yet above the shouts and screams, laughter and mockery, sales, arguments, singing, and chatter, Jemima could hear something else. Perhaps on the next street over, perhaps on the street on the other side of that, there was a noise throbbing in the base of her skull. When she concentrated, she could make out drums. The sound of marching feet. Cheers and shouting.

Her curiosity piqued, Jemima left the spot where she had been standing and moved towards where the noise was coming from.

It wasn't hard to find; with every step that she took toward the kerfuffle, the noise became clearer, until she stumbled out of an alleyway into what felt like a wall of sound.

A military parade was striding down the street, men in their uniforms led by a set of musicians. Drummers led at the front, four in each of the three rows, drumming out a march. The crowds lining the street on either side cheered and shouted support for the men who had been, only a few days before, defending Britain's honor against the rebellious Napoleon.

Jemima could not help but stare in anger and disgust.

She had heard much about the war in France, as everyone had. Had borrowed her father's newspapers each day, had followed the movement of troops, the list of the lost, and the cries of victory in the black ink.

How did the country stand it? Watching their men return to pain and illness, with no support and no help to acclimatize them back to their country?

It was not the soldiers' fault, of course. Jemima looked into the exhausted faces of the men who passed her. They had served their country and done so admirably. She could find no fault with them.

But these wars in France—when would they end?

She had signed petitions and attempted to talk much with her family about her passion for supporting soldiers after the war—yet she had never before seen any of the actual men from the battlefield.

Many men had scars across their faces, and one man seemed to have burns on his forehead. They had healed well, however, and he beamed up at the world, seemingly uncaring that his visage had been altered.

The soldiers were all staring up the street as if they could barely believe they were there, accepting the cheers and celebration their attendance seemed to warrant from the crowds—except one.

Jemima noticed him immediately. He was not near the front of the parade and wore more medals than the others. His uniform was neat and tidy, though not spotless, and a mop of jet-black hair was untamed. His dark sideburns swept down past his ears, and a sharp jawline jutted out in a determined fashion. He was the only man amongst them not striding out in time with the beat of the twelve drummers.

Under his left arm was a crutch. He limped forward, eyes never darting to the adoring crowd. It was as if he was alone, marching home after a long day.

Jemima could not take her eyes from him.

How had this man found himself in the army? What battles had he seen? What struggles had he known; what suffering had brought him to the point of leaning on a wooden crutch to walk?

Her curiosity, once enflamed, was difficult to quench, and her eyes ate up the sight of him greedily, battling with her instant dislike of his uniform.

Her stomach lurched as the man approached her slowly but surely. He was tall, she could see that now. Taller than she. Taller even than Papa.

Jemima knew she needed to take a step backward to ensure his crutch would have enough berth to support him—but her feet did not seem able to move. She could not step away from him.

Unable to completely ignore the woman standing in his way, the soldier turned his head ever so slightly to the left, and their eyes met.

Jemima's breath caught in her throat. She had been determined to ignore him, but as soon as their eyes met, she knew she would never forget him.

The man's eyes were dark, darker than she had ever seen before, yet there seemed to be such a depth and a fierceness to them. As though a spark of lightning had pulsed through them and into her. Jemima's hand involuntarily moved from her side to her chest as she felt her heart race.

The drummers were somehow louder, now matching the odd and uncomfortable beating of her heart.

She had never felt this strange feeling before, but she knew enough about the world to give it its rightful name: desire.

She desired him. Jemima's mouth was dry, her heart still thumping wildly, but her instinct to reach out and touch the soldier was rising in her chest.

She had to be close to him. It did not make any sense. One

look. Their eyes had met on a street populated by hundreds.

It did not matter. Something had occurred between them, something she did not understand but could no longer ignore.

The soldier's eyes widened as if he, too, was aware of the strangeness of the feeling which had just swept between them—confusion and lust all mingled into a strange concoction that was certainly making her lightheaded.

His mouth opened as if he was about to speak to her, yet no words came out.

Jemima willed her feet to move, commanded them silently to remove herself from her present position, yet closer and closer the gentleman came, and there was absolutely no change in her location. If she did not move within the next few seconds, then she was going to be mowed down by a military march!

Despite the strangeness of the feeling between them, and despite what appeared to be a complete inability of her body to obey even the simplest of commands, Jemima was suddenly able to take a short step backward. It was a miracle she did not step onto anyone's toes as the crowd gathered was quite substantial.

Thankfully, however, no toes were mangled, and Jemima breathed a sigh of relief.

She looked up once more at the gentleman with the crutch and gasped when she realized just how close he now was. If she reached out her hand, if she just extended her fingers, she would be able to touch him, would feel the roughness of his skin …

His gaze had not returned to its deadpan stare ahead of him. Now he was so close to her, Jemima realized he was in quite real danger of losing his balance.

The soldier stumbled, and before Jemima knew what was happening, he was lying across her, the two of them in a heap on the ground.

CHAPTER THREE

"BLAST YOU, YOU couldn't just move over?"
The soldier's words were brusque and harsh and spoken close to her ear as they lay disheveled on the ground. It was wet beneath her, and Jemima could feel the damp seeping into her gown.

He was incredibly close, closer than she could ever have imagined. Closer than any gentleman had ever been to her. He was lying on top of her—in public.

A brass button scraped across her cheek, and as she tried to take a deep breath, she took in his scent—deep, musky, and with a hint of something that could only be gunpowder.

She had not mistaken herself minutes earlier. It was desire coursing through her veins. His masculine scent, his weight upon her, in the most intimate of circumstances...

Jemima felt a warmth spread through her that she had never felt before. But she had to speak. She could not merely lie here!

"I do apologize," she said in a low voice, all breath knocked out of her by the fall.

Strong hands reached down each side of her, and the weight on her chest suddenly lifted as the soldier attempted to push himself upright.

Her view now cleared, Jemima suddenly realized half of the street seemed to be peering at her. She could already hear some of the murmurs.

"Straight down he fell, by Jove!"

"It was almost as if she wanted him to fall on her!"

"What a harlot…in only a gown, in this weather!"

She certainly regretted her rash decision to push Arabella away, pelisse and all, now she was lying on the damp ground with mud splattered about her.

Despite the soldier's best efforts to remove himself from her and stand upright, it was clear he could not without some assistance. Jemima saw his crutch, fallen just out of reach of where she lay. He was muttering curses under his breath as he sat painfully on his haunches, stretching out a hand in the hope of being able to reach it.

"I can reach it for—" Jemima attempted to say. It was the least she could do, after all. What had possessed her to stand in the way of the soldier? Why had her feet not moved?

"Let me," he said decidedly in a harsh voice.

He had pushed himself up, leaning and reaching out for his crutch—but Jemima had instinctively reached also, and her fingers brushed past that of the gentleman.

He pulled back with a hiss under his breath. She had felt it, too. Jemima gazed at him, stunned.

"Let me help you," he said gruffly, as though nothing had occurred between them.

Jemima's head was in a daze. Had he felt it, too? Surely it was not possible for her to feel that alone. The rabble of the street roared in her ears as her pulse continued to quicken.

But she would not permit him to help her. A stranger, a soldier no less, reach out and touch her? It would be scandalous!

"I do not need your help!" Jemima's voice was as firm as she could make it, given the circumstances. "But when I do require the help of a soldier who can't look where he is going, I shall be the first to let you know!"

He laughed. "And much good it will do you! I see no reason to lend a hand now."

"Lending a hand is not what I require," Jemima said curtly, rising to her feet.

"And not what I am offering," snapped the man.

Jemima shivered slightly in the chilly breeze. "A gentleman would have been polite enough to accept my apology, but now you are proven to be no such thing, I have no qualms at all at leaving you here in your own mess."

The soldier struggled once more to reach his crutch, whilst muttering—under his breath but clearly audible to Jemima, "God save me from women throwing themselves at my feet..."

Jemima's color heightened. The arrogance of the man! "I attempted to move out of the way, and I did, so do not blame me if you could not take your eyes from me! Do not flatter yourself that I was in any way attempting to capture your attention, I-I have more important things to do than speak to soldiers!"

"Really?" he said bitterly, "With a dress that crimson, I could have mistaken you for an infantryman!"

She stared down at the man, incensed. His hat had fallen off and had become lost somewhere in the crowd—Jemima suspected a pickpocket but could not be sure—and mud had splattered across his crimson jacket. Wild, jet-black hair skimmed over his brow and across his eyes, and he raised a hand to sweep it back so that he could gain a clear look at Jemima.

His frown disappeared slowly, but Jemima did not wait to hear more from him. Brushing as much mud as she could from her gown, she turned on her heels and took a step forward.

"Wait."

Jemima could not help but pause. There was no anger in the words the soldier had just uttered; instead, there was an element of pleading. The words were spoken softly enough not to be noticeable by the disappointed crowd, who had seemed to expect a physical brawl and had now drifted away to follow the parade.

Jemima had not noticed until now that the men had marched on. The drums were now distant. Strange, though. The sound of a second set of drums were still audible, and she could not comprehend from whence they came.

It was only after taking another steadying breath that she realized it was her own heart not ceasing its tattoo on her rib cage.

Slowly, she turned her head to look over her shoulder. The soldier had managed to reach his crutch and was righting himself. The sight of his face caused her to turn around fully to face him.

He was smiling. The expression utterly transformed his features from a scowling man one would easily pass in a crowd, to a remarkably handsome gentleman.

Soldier. Jemima tried to remind herself that she was a lady and he just a soldier she had knocked into the street. There was no need to be excited. No need to hope for anything more.

"You are a blunt little thing, aren't you?"

There was no malevolence in his voice, but Jemima could detect a hint of mischievousness—which, she thought, would make a pleasant change from the dullards she had been forced to smile at every social occasion.

"Little?" She replied haughtily. "Has the fall affected your eyes as well as your tongue? I do not think that I would be considered little anywhere."

She spoke the honest truth; she was taller than all her sisters and her stepmother, an unfortunate trait when one was searching for a husband.

But before the soldier could reply, he reached his crutch and pulled himself to his feet. Jemima was reminded once again that he was remarkably tall himself. Taller by a good two or three inches.

A smile broke out on her face, which seemed to give his smile heart.

"Bluntness is something you have truly committed to, isn't it?" the soldier said honestly. His left arm was now securely tucked over his crutch as he leaned on it for support.

Jemima laughed darkly. "It has been noted by a few of my acquaintances. I suppose I never really learned the secret of lying politely, as ladies are supposed to."

The soldier's face twisted suddenly with something like sadness, but Jemima could not be exactly sure—it was a mere flicker, and then it was gone. He wiped his right hand on his black trousers, smearing them with mud, then bowed as best as he could with his left leg immobile.

"Captain Rotherham," he said. When Jemima said nothing, he spoke again, more hesitantly. "Captain Hugh Rotherham."

This was ridiculous, Jemima told herself. This was not how young ladies met elegant bachelors! Falling over each other into a muddy London street!

Still, there was nothing to be done save following Society's niceties. Jemima curtseyed. "Miss Jemima Fitzroy."

Captain Rotherham's smile lit up the street. "Miss Fitzroy, I must admit it is an absolute delight to meet you."

Jemima flushed, heat seeping through her. What nonsense. No gentleman had ever suffered her company, and she had no wish to be mocked. "I have already apologized, Captain Rotherham, I see no reason to tease me after I have tried to make amends."

The flush in her face deepening, Jemima turned away and began to walk back toward her home. Enough of this nonsense. The air was chill, and her gown was damp. All she wished to do was return home and change, though it would of course necessitate seeing Caroline again.

Drat.

"Miss Fitzroy!" Captain Rotherham's voice called after her, and she could hear his footsteps and crutch following her. Then, "Dang and blast, the march has moved on! I've been left behind!"

Jemima picked up her feet and quickened her pace, but it was not enough to escape Captain Rotherham, determined as he was. His hand closed on her shoulder, and he twisted her round, the smile gone from his face.

"Your antics have delayed me such that I shall miss official presentations!"

Jemima reached up and forcibly removed Captain Rotherham's hand from her arm, ignoring the part of her that wished it would remain. She could not permit herself to be, be manhandled like this!

There was now a slightly damp and muddy handprint on the right shoulder of her gown—something Jemima knew would be the devil to remove.

"You cannot force another apology out of me," Jemima said. "I do not think you should even be receiving the small and pitiful thanks a November crowd can offer you. In any case, I have done all I can, and if you insist on finding offense where none is intended, then this brief acquaintance is at an end."

Jemima did not just walk away; she stormed away.

Was she always to be mocked, to be disbelieved, to be ignored when she spoke the truth? Her heart sank as she remembered the scene she had left at home: Caroline and Dr. Stuart Walsingham's engagement, her stepmother's speech, her outburst…

"Now see here!"

Jemima was not entirely sure how Captain Rotherham managed it, but she was startled to find he had somehow gone ahead of her and now stood before her blocking her path. Her stomach lurched once more. It was most disobliging, and she really shouldn't be talking to a gentleman—nor a stranger—she had not been introduced to.

She opened her mouth in anger, but he spoke before she could.

"I know I have been rude, and I know moreover it was not your fault that I…that we fell. And so, you'll get an apology out of me, Miss Fitzroy, and that's a good deal more than most get, so I hope you'll be grateful for it! But I have fought for my country, young lady, and that is something few women can boast, so perhaps you should show a little more respect when you speak to me!"

Jemima could see that he was flushed, a medley, surely, of

embarrassment and irritation and perhaps a little fury. He had the same temper she did, and it roused something in her that no other man ever had.

Apology, indeed. Apologizing in such a way!

Jemima's smile was thin. "Your lackluster apology is accepted."

She turned to go, but before she could make a move, Captain Rotherham said, "Wait."

It was a word softly spoken yet contained more warmth and real feeling than any word which had passed between them.

Jemima's eyes flickered up to his, and once again she marveled at their darkness, at their depth, at the intensity with which they were being directed at her. At her. The Fitzroy always lost in a crowd.

Captain Rotherham took a step toward her and lowered his voice so the rabble of people that passed them on the street could not attend. "You do not seek to ask me why I know that it was not your fault we fell?"

She tried to speak but found her mouth too dry. She swallowed. "No. I would force no confidences from you."

Captain Rotherham smiled gently. "Then you are different from most women that I have met."

"It has taken you this long to comprehend?" asked Jemima quietly.

He appeared to be just as off-balance now as when he had been sprawled in the mud. "I do not blame you for the fall. On my honor. I will be brave enough to admit to myself that the real reason for my losing my balance and toppling over like a fool was because I was distracted."

"Distracted?"

Captain Rotherham took another step forward, and now Jemima could almost feel his breath upon her forehead they were so close. It blossomed in the winter air. Her spine tingled.

"Distracted by you, of course."

For a moment, they just stood there, gazes locked. If she had tried, Jemima was unsure whether she would have been able to break the connection, but of course, she had no wish to.

Captain Rotherham. Never before had a man bewitched her so utterly.

The more she looked into his eyes, the deeper she seemed to fall into them. His broad shoulders were steady now, and he gazed at her with the same intensity. As though he knew what she was thinking. As though he could see her imagination, in which he pulled her into his arms and kissed her, the fury and irritation of their interactions poured out into desire.

Jemima swallowed. She should not think such thoughts. It was wicked. It was indecent.

It was precisely what she wished he would do.

And then a gentleman in a hurry pushed between them, and the moment was broken.

"I do beg your pardon, I'm terribly late!"

Jemima knew she should say something, but for some reason, absolutely every single word in the English language had completely escaped her. She was wholly incapable of uttering a syllable.

"Miss Fitzroy," said Captain Rotherham with a slight tremor in his voice, "if you are not engaged for anything this very moment, it would give me great pleasure if you would accompany me to the nearest park and sit with me awhile."

"Sit with you?" repeated Jemima. "Sit with you. Sit."

Captain Rotherham clearly was unsure whether she meant this last remark as a question. "Yes, sit with me and talk for a while." Once again, he took a step forward and closed the distance between them. "You are by far the most interesting and beautiful woman I have ever met, and I would be unwise and senseless to let you walk away from me."

Despite the winter chill, heat was blossoming through every inch of Jemima's body.

"You are by far the most interesting and beautiful woman I have ever met, and I would be unwise and senseless to let you walk away from

me."

Was the man in earnest?

Surely, he was not. No man had ever thought those senti-ments about her, let alone spoken them.

Jemima hesitated. He did not have the appearance of a liar. He appeared to be trustworthy, handsome, honorable...

She knew she should return home; knew her family was probably worried about her; knew it was madness to wander off with a gentleman she had just met, especially as he was a soldier—and yet...

"No," she said abruptly, her decision made despite her desire. "No, I am sorry, Captain Rotherham, but I have no desire to sit and be stunned at how brave you were at conquering another's country. As I said, I have other things to do."

He may have attempted to argue with her, but Jemima could not tell. Without a backward glance, she turned and strode into the crowd.

CHAPTER FOUR

"I JUST DO not think it will be possible to have my bridal trousseau ready in time." Caroline shook her head. "Mama, whatever shall we do?"

"Ah, child, we will simply have to do our best." Selina smiled benevolently at her daughter. "And you know your papa will do absolutely all that he can to give you what you desire. Do not be afraid to ask."

Jemima rolled her eyes. Thankfully, as she was seated at the opposite end of the dining table, her insolence went unnoticed.

"And the church has an opening on Christmas Day!" Caroline was still speaking in raptures as they finished their pudding. "I know 'tis unusual, but I just cannot wait to be his wife. Walsingham. Mrs. Walsingham! I have already spoken with the reverend, and he has said that…"

Like any other occasion when Caroline was speaking, Jemima allowed the words to simply wash over her, paying little heed or attention to what was actually being discussed.

It was often easier, and her temper was less likely to be roused, and she could dwell on things that mattered to her, even if her family could not be drawn into a discussion on just what Napoleon would do after losing at the Battle of Leipzig.

"Did you go?"

Startled, Jemima saw Arabella looking at her with an accusing eye.

"Go?" She replied blankly, spoon halfway to her mouth.

"To the parade. The march. Mrs. Castle mentioned it as we came into dinner, the soldiers' parade that went through town today. Did you go?"

Jemima swallowed. She was not a liar, it was not in her nature, but she hardly wished to give her family further reasons to despair at her behavior.

It did not appear to matter, however. Arabella knew her too well.

She sighed heavily. "I knew it would be so, yet I had hoped you had kept away. Jemima, how long will you go against public opinion? The war with Napoleon is almost over, surely, and then we can go back to our lives—you can return to your life!"

"What life?" Jemima snorted. "Waiting for Papa to start parading me around Society like a prize mare?"

"And all of my sisters shall be my bridesmaids!" Caroline's voice broke through to their conversation for a moment.

Arabella's head turned to the other end of the table, and then she looked back at Jemima, her voice low. "Just tell me that you were not...*seen*...by anyone of our acquaintance."

The face of the soldier flashed into Jemima's mind: those dark eyes, that furrowed brow, the crutch on one side keeping him upright, the strange feelings that just one glance could stir in her, sensations so forbidden, so dark...

"My word, Jemima, who did you see there?"

Arabella's shocked voice broke into her reverie, and Jemima started. Her cheeks were flushed, and she put down her spoon hurriedly. Her fruit cake covered in cream lay forgotten.

"No one," she said quietly. "I saw no one of our acquaintance there."

And this was not necessarily a complete lie, Jemima told herself the next day.

After all, she had never set eyes on that man, as she was now calling him in her thoughts, before yesterday. He could not really be described as an acquaintance.

"Jemima?"

Indeed, apart from his name, she knew nothing about him, save that he was a soldier and so was part and parcel of the war effort which she desired to end. What else was there to be known?

"Jemima, can you hear me?"

Jemima blinked. She was standing in the breakfast room with Sophia staring at her with concern on her face.

Her little sister moved forward and placed a hand on her arm. "Jemima, are you quite well?"

Jemima swallowed. "Quite well, I assure you. A trick of the light meant something caught my eye, but it is gone. It was just a passing glint. It was nothing."

Sophia, too young to disbelieve her eldest sister, smiled with relief. She had adorned an orange cotton gown with a beautiful Spencer jacket and was evidently heading off somewhere.

No doubt with Caroline, Jemima thought bitterly. Off to select more delightful gowns for her trousseau.

"I thought you thinking on a gentleman!" Sophia said with a laugh, before scampering off.

Jemima colored but said nothing. What could she say? How could she explain such an inexplicable event as that which had occurred?

Love at first sight?

Nonsense. Jemima had never believed in such nonsense, and she was not about to now. Even as she got left behind by her family, too absorbed in Caroline's joy to notice her own prickly feelings of being left out.

Although Arabella was about to open her mouth to question further, she paused when she saw Jemima's expression. Her pelisse was over her arm, and her favorite day dress in mauve with a deep purple print had been adorned with a rather beautiful brooch—one Jemima was almost sure was her own.

Not that ownership of trifles really occurred in the Fitzroy family, not with six sisters; if it existed, it was borrowed.

"I'll see you later then, Jemima," said Arabella slowly, and she left the breakfast room.

Any other day, the discomforting conversation which had just taken place would have irritated Jemima to the core and caused her probably to snap at her sisters—but not today.

She had read in the newspaper just that morning that there was to be what was being termed an "anti-war rally" by some, a "pacifism meeting" by others, and a "damned nuisance" by still more.

Jemima had never given her promise to her father about not attending such a thing, but she knew none of her family understood. They did not even try.

Today was the first day the family's attention had been so distracted she may actually be able to attend. To see what others thought about the war. To hear from soldiers whether they wished to return to France.

Today was the day that Caroline had her wedding invitations engraved. Jemima snorted, alone in the breakfast room. A most important day indeed.

It did not take long for her to find the location of the gathering, printed inconspicuously at the bottom of the article, and even if she had not remembered it exactly, she would have had absolutely no difficulty in finding it.

Shouts and cries were emanating from one particular street, and despite the heavy fall of snow the previous night, there were countless people teeming the streets. Some were carrying banners, and one woman who pushed past Jemima was wearing a white sash.

Never before had she ever encountered anyone who understood her passionate desire to see all the soldiers return home and stay here, in England. Was this it, perhaps? Was she about to find people amongst whom she did not have to pretend?

Jemima looked around, bright-eyed, and as she turned the corner, she saw two men standing on a large box that put them head and shoulders above the crowd gathered there.

"...at once!" one of them was shouting. "It simply cannot continue, and the ceasefire which can bring hope and peace to our once happy nation must occur at the swiftest opportunity! Only by joining together with amity and true friendship can the war in France come to an end!"

Cheers and applause rang out, and Jemima clapped her hands together. Was there anything so isolating as believing you could be the only person to think one way—and anything so freeing as discovering you were just one of many?

The second man on the box was now speaking. "And we are not alone in this! All those who signed the Loughborough Petition stand alongside us, and there are still more in other countries who also cry out for the end of violence!"

More cheers echoed around her. Jemima could feel her heart pounding, almost audible for those around her she was sure, so heavy in her ears it was, like the pounding of the ocean's tide against the cliffs.

Surely this war could not continue as it was, when so many people here stood against it!

She turned her head around to take in the sight of so many people—shopkeepers, gentlemen, a few children running around their heels. A woman over there wore such a rich fur that she was surely nobility of some kind, and over there—

The heartbeat Jemima had been hearing in her ears stopped and then started again.

Captain Hugh Rotherham.

The man who had toppled her to the ground—or she had toppled, she had almost forgotten which—was standing right there, his gaze rapt on the speaker on the box. And he was in uniform.

Leaving little thought for the consequences, Jemima pushed past those between them, and within twenty seconds of first espying him in the crowd, found herself before him.

"What in God's name do you think you are doing here?"

It was, perhaps, not the best of opening sentences for a conversation.

The man's eyebrows raised. "This is a free country, madam—free thanks to the bravery of soldiers who keep this country free of tyranny, may I add. 'Tis no crime to stand here."

"No crime!" Jemima hissed. "Do you think this is a good idea, standing here in a crowd of people who hate war, in the bright red uniform of a soldier?"

She blushed at her own words. The last thing she wanted was for Hugh to believe she was such a person, unsupportive of the common soldier.

But he laughed. "Not good pacifists are they if my safety is in danger by merely being here. I bring no ill will, I am just...curious."

Captain Rotherham stared at her, and Jemima's conscience pinched her.

She was not supposed to accost gentlemen in the street for simply standing where they wished to. She knew that. She had been raised a lady and should comport herself such.

But Captain Rotherham did something to her. Something she did not understand. His presence drew her to him, no matter what she told herself was right and proper, and there was a flicker of concern in her heart for the man she had spent but ten minutes with until this moment.

"In truth," he said quietly. "Curiosity of the rally was not the reason I have come here. I would not typically admit this to another soul, let alone the soul who has piqued my interest."

It took Jemima a moment to understand what on earth he was talking about. Then her cheeks flamed red.

Piqued his interest—her?

"It was in hope of seeing you that I have traveled across London to this bizarre meeting," the captain said quietly below the hubbub, "and my recklessness has been rewarded."

Reckless indeed. Jemima hardly knew where to look. No gentleman had ever been interested in her. Interested in her sisters, true, and therefore willing to speak with her to elicit their goodwill.

But speak to her? Wish for her company?

It was unheard of. It was madness.

And that was the only reason, Jemima told herself, that warmth was spreading throughout her body. She was flattered, that was all. It was natural to be so.

It did not mean anything.

"But…" she stammered, wishing she was more coherent. "But what if you are not welcome?"

For some reason, she did not know what to do with her hands, so she clasped them behind her.

It did not seem real, that this man she had encountered by chance just one day before was here again.

Why did he seem to have such an effect on her? Despite the cold air around them, she felt uncomfortably warm. Her hands were tingling, and it was not the cold. Her gaze could not leave him.

Captain Rotherham spread his arms around him. "You appear to be the sole person who is troubled by my presence."

"That is because they are more polite than I," said Jemima with a dark smile. "You are the very thing we discuss, do you not see?"

"I am just a man!" Captain Rotherham said, and now his words appeared more irritated. "And a man who was given orders, which he obeyed. Nothing more."

Jemima laughed unbelievingly. "Sir, you are a man who brings war!"

"And what benefit does this rally have?" the captain bit back. "I see no collections of money for widows and orphans, no understanding of what it is like to be part of a battle, no true human feeling for any of us who have come back!"

Jemima could feel the heat within her rising, and though it was mainly anger, there seemed to be something about the captain's physical presence that seemed to incense her even further.

Besides, she could not disagree with a word he said. She had not considered those elements, and she was certain no one else at the rally had either.

It was most discomforting to be proven wrong, and so she did not admit it. "You should have kept up with your parade yesterday," Jemima said cuttingly. "It is there, and there alone that you will receive your thanks. This is a place to hear exactly what we can do to end this suffering!"

Now the captain was shaking his head. "Do you really think that you can end a war by standing around in a street and complaining about it?"

"'Tis better than doing nothing!" Jemima shot back.

"'Tis the same thing!"

He looked truly aggrieved, and Jemima found a spark of disappointment in her heart. They were such different people. If only they had more in common...but no. She must not think that way. She should not be thinking of him at all.

"But I did not come here to quarrel with you, Miss Fitzroy."

The sound of her name made Jemima start. "I...I did not think you knew my name."

Captain Rotherham smiled, and she was reminded unwillingly that he really was a handsome man. "Of course, I do, you told it to me only yesterday. Now, what other topic shall we discuss? You?"

"Me?" Jemima scowled. "You don't want to talk to me—and I don't want to talk to you!"

"Don't you?"

Jemima swallowed. The captain had a rather unfortunate way of saying precisely what she did not wish him to say—and for looking at her as though he knew her, which was of course impossible.

If only he did not look so dashing in his red coat and brass buttons. The medals had gone, perhaps only brought out for the march.

Still, he cut a very gallant figure. Jemima was not able to ignore the other ladies in the crowd who were glancing enviously in their direction.

As though she owned him. As though he was courting her.

She swallowed. She had to leave. "I just thought I would give you the recommendation of leaving, that is all. Good day to you."

Strange reflexes were urging her to stay, but she overrode them and turned away—but a hand on her arm prevented her from going any further.

"I asked you yesterday if you wanted to go on a walk with me, to a park." Captain Rotherham's voice was low and serious, yet Jemima was able to catch every syllable, even over the loud shouts of the rally. "You said no. I am asking you again."

Jemima opened her mouth to instantly reply in the negative, but her eyes were caught by his dark ones, and she stopped.

When was the last time that she had had a conversation of this length with a gentleman—with any man?

All she had done was berate him, yet he wanted to spend more time with her. What did he see in her that no others did? That she herself did not?

What harm could it do?

"Certainly, Captain Rotherham," Jemima said matter of factly, certain she may regret this decision. "I will certainly walk with you. Which park do you consider most pleasant?"

Their five-minute walk to Hyde Park was taken in silence, awkwardness on both sides keeping them from speaking. Captain Rotherham was unable to walk at any great pace, wincing slightly with every step that he took.

"If you would not mind, we'll sit here," he said as they passed their first bench.

"Not at all." Jemima silently willed herself to be less obstinate and inelegant. He was just a gentleman. A gentleman who captured her breath whenever she looked at him.

He sat on the left of the bench, his injured leg as far from her as it was possible to be; his body, however, was turned toward her, and Jemima could not help but be highly aware of the short distance between his hand and hers as the two palms both laid on the bench.

If he just reached out...if her hand were to move ever so slightly.

No. Hoping to distract herself from the potent presence of the man, Jemima looked around her. This was one of her favorite benches in Hyde Park, beside the lake and, in the summer, covered by a canopy of leaves, which rustled in any breeze that moved by.

This being November, however, it was a different scene. The lake was gray, almost silver, and there was no cover above. The trees curled upwards, inelegantly yet majestic, waiting for spring to return.

She had never come here with a gentleman, never sat with a young man whom she had not even known from Adam a mere day before.

Jemima shivered.

"You are cold," said Captain Rotherham.

Jemima turned to look at him with an argument on her tongue, but it was stayed by the smile on his face. Still, she could not allow herself to giggle like a foolish chit on the floor of Almack's. That was not who she was.

"Do not concern yourself," said Jemima in an abrupt tone. What was she thinking? Walking out here with a complete stranger? Who did she think she was trying to impress? And yet, there was something about this man—something that had made her accept his offer of a walk.

Something that made her time with him...different.

Captain Rotherham laughed. "Where would we be without our British spirit? Come, Miss Fitzroy, it is laughable you should sit there cold whilst I wear such a warm coat."

With those words, he pulled his jacket off and, despite her loud and clear protestations, wrapped her snugly into it.

Despite Jemima's words, the jacket was very welcome. Not

only did it immediately warm her, but it also meant she was inadvertently able to see a great more of Captain Rotherham.

Her assumption of his broad shoulders was confirmed as she saw his white linen shirt stretched tight across his chest. He was not wearing any cravat at his neck; a smattering of dark curls could be seen at his open shirt.

Jemima lifted her face to look at Captain Rotherham. He was smiling, and the warmth of his smile was quite startling. Jemima could not help but blush.

"I like your boldness," said Captain Rotherham in a low voice, his hand moving slightly so that it rested gently over hers. "Yet I can see this is not something that you have ever done...ever wanted to do before. Walking with a gentleman, I mean. Am I right?"

Jemima nodded, not trusting her voice to speak. How was it possible for such a man to see right into her heart?

Her hand was covered in his, a weighty yet welcome presence.

What was she doing?

"Interesting," mused Captain Rotherham, "I must admit it surprises me. You are so beautiful."

"I?" Jemima spluttered, drawing her fingers away ever so slightly out of the reach of his own. "I think whatever damaged your leg must have damaged your eyesight, too!"

As soon as the words had escaped her mouth, she regretted them. Curse her blasted tongue! It was always too hasty to speak, with none of the softness and care her sisters displayed.

"I apologize," said Jemima swiftly, her face now burning for the dual reason of embarrassment and the yearning to further examine Captain Rotherham's physique. "Please do not heed my words, I speak without thought, and it is most disgraceful that—"

"Now, you can stop that," said Captain Rotherham, nodding at a passerby in a similar uniform to his own. "Miss Fitzroy, it is my deepest wish that you do not feel you have to be shy of talking to me about anything."

"Anything?" Jemima arched an eyebrow suspiciously. She leaned back into the bench so that the distance between them was minutely increased.

This was not a good idea. She should have gone with Caroline to the dratted engravers, followed Sophia and Arabella into town to examine gloves and such things.

She should not be seated here on a bench, speaking plainly to a man she had just met!

But it did not feel wrong. It felt right, more right than anything else ever had.

Even if her imagination was offering her images of Captain Rotherham, pressed up against her, covering her body on the bench as he rained kisses down her neck...

The real Captain Rotherham laughed, his black hair falling over his eyes once more.

Jemima was tempted to push it back from his eyes but resisted the temptation. It was scandalous enough that she was even here. It would never do for her to start being intimate with him.

"Anything," repeated Captain Rotherham. He shifted himself slightly on the bench, and Jemima found to her surprise that he had moved marginally toward her. His hand brushed hers on the bench. "For example, I do not wish you to try to ignore my crutch, nor be embarrassed by it."

Jemima nodded slowly. "I can see how that could be unpleasant—for all involved. How did your injury occur?"

Darkness, and not just his dark hair, now swept across the face of Captain Rotherham. It was such a sudden change, Jemima was startled, and she cursed her own bluntness for offending a man who must have seen worse things in battle than she could possibly imagine.

"Forgive me," said Jemima hurriedly, "I misspoke, I forgot myself—"

"No, no," Captain Rotherham said gently, but with a degree of tension in his voice. "You were bound to ask, and I do not blame you for it. I would rather your thoughts be voiced to me than you be forced to self-censure."

He paused for a moment, and as that moment lengthened, Jemima wondered whether or not he was actually going to speak again, or whether he was merely gazing out into the distance.

But when he spoke once more, she realized that Captain Rotherham was not seeing the lake before them lined with spindly trees, nor the children playing with their governesses as they fed the ducks. No, he was seeing a much darker picture of a land far from where they sat.

"It is a terrible thing, war," Captain Rotherham said finally. "It is not something I would wish on anyone, especially a young lady like yourself, Miss Fitzroy. War can rip humanity from a man's very self and forbids him to act in charity and gentleness. The man who did this to me," and he used his crutch to point at his left leg, immobile and awkward, "had clearly seen just as much war and devastation as I had, but it had...affected him slightly differently."

"Affected him?" Jemima whispered, barely aware that she had spoken aloud. She unconsciously leaned toward him. "I have read much about the war, but never having met a soldier before, it has been impossible for me to tell whether or not the newspapers have done what they always do and exaggerate beyond the credence of truth."

Captain Rotherham raised an eyebrow. "Your quick intellect does you credit. But they are right, in the main. Many of us have injuries beyond that which one can see, and his was one that affected him greatly. I was considered an imminent threat, and so he acted accordingly. I had gone down to a village in search of water, and he happened to be standing near the village well."

Jemima could picture it, a French village, shutters at the windows, and brightly painted houses lining the roads. A well, a bucket waiting patiently beside it, to be used by whoever required water. And a man in a crimson jacket approaching a man in a navy jacket...

Captain Rotherham's words returned her to the present.

"And that was that. My injury was severe enough to remove me to a hospital, but not severe enough to return me to England before my regiment was scheduled to winter here. And so, I waited for five months in a chair whilst my comrades went out and defended our country."

It was not difficult for Jemima to detect the bitterness in his words. "But you survived," she said quietly, unable to hide her true thoughts, her feelings of relief and gratitude that he had lived, and so had been able to meet her on that dirty street. "Many did not."

"A shell of me survived," said Captain Rotherham candidly. "Not as I was."

Jemima fell silent as she stared at the soldier seated beside her.

She knew such an obvious stare would be considered rude, but she and Captain Rotherham had transgressed so many rules of decorum that she felt no shame in breaking this one.

There was certainly a darkness in him. Not only in his eyes and in his hair, but in his very soul.

So, this was what a soldier was after he returned from battle. Her anger at warfare and all it held for men such as this deepened.

Then he smiled, his dark eyes flashing. "It was why I could not wrench my eyes from you."

"Me?" Jemima said stunned. "Why on earth? The closest I have been to France is my French dressmakers!"

Captain Rotherham laughed. "Not because I thought you had any French battle experience. Miss Fitzroy, you may calm yourself! No, I could not help but stare at your eyes. The more I gazed into them, the more I realized you have suffered great hurt as well. You have been let down by people, ignored by them, perhaps slighted by them by their disregard of your opinions."

Jemima's mouth fell open. "How on earth…"

Captain Rotherham shrugged. "When one has experienced it, one learns to recognize it. And what I asked myself was, what has a woman of twenty—"

"One and twenty," corrected Jemima automatically.

She hated herself for doing it as soon as the words had left her lips, but she could not help it. She felt painfully that extra year that pushed her from being a new blossom in Society to a faded rose that had seen better days.

"A woman of one and twenty experienced that could have brought her so much sadness? So much isolation. So much in common with a man like myself."

Jemima looked into his eyes and saw such understanding, such compassion, such lust that she could no longer deny it.

It made her blush just to think it.

She was attracted to Captain Rotherham.

There was a stirring in her no other man had created, a pull in her navel that was drawing her to him in a way that she could not—would not—resist.

Captain Rotherham's gaze moved down to her mouth. A jolt surged through her, one she could not control.

If he was not careful, she was going to move into his arms and place her lips on his, forcing them apart to take what she wanted…

They stared at each other.

Jemima licked her lips unconsciously and saw the captain's jaw tighten.

He wanted her. It felt wonderful to be so desired, to have such control over a man. She had no idea where it came from, no idea how to wield it—but she had some power over him.

The same power he had over her.

The air seemed to crackle with the repressed desire that neither of them seemed willing to take advantage of. Jemima certainly wouldn't; she was a lady. It was for him to kiss her, to whisper sweet nothings in her ear, to make the tingle down her spine move to the rest of her body…

And it was just not just his dazzling good looks. Captain Rotherham understood her, recognized a kindred spirit, and she had not even mentioned a word of her family: her loss of her mother, the stepmother that did not seem to understand her, the countless sisters all demanding attention from their parents, and the gentlemen that passed them, and her father...

Her father was standing directly behind Captain Rotherham!

"Jemima Fitzroy!"

Jemima stood up frantically as Captain Rotherham swung round to see who had spoken.

Arthur Fitzroy, dressed in a dark green overcoat with his collar pulled up against his ears, stormed forward and stopped in front of his eldest daughter.

"Jemima Fitzroy, where in Heaven's name have you been? Have you no thought at all within that selfish head, have you no consideration for the feelings of others? Your mother has been frantic, Sophia has been crying this last hour, and if Caroline ever manages to forgive you, then I shall be very much surprised! Did you completely neglect to remember that you had promised to meet us after the engravers at the bakery to discuss the wedding cake?"

Jemima was not entirely sure how her father had said all of this in one breath, but he had managed it.

Scarlet with embarrassment, she tried to speak quickly and under her breath. "She is not my mother, Sophia cries every afternoon for some reason or another, and Caroline's engagement ball will be more than enough to satisfy her! No," Jemima interrupted her father before he could speak again, "you know these facts to be true, Papa, so do not attempt to dissemble with me."

"The last thing I shall do is argue with you," said her father, the frown on his face darkening, tugging at his collar to keep his ears from the cold, "but when we get home—"

"Mr. Fitzroy?"

Jemima's father turned to face the soldier who was standing, somewhat awkwardly, with a crutch underneath his left arm. The captain bowed.

Only then did she remember the warmth she was currently enjoying was thanks to the captain's jacket around her shoulders.

"My name is Captain Hugh Rotherham," he said with a smile for Jemima, "and I must bear all the blame for Miss Fitzroy's absence. She was good enough to attend to me when I fell in the street, and she would not leave me until she had been assured of my health. She brought me to this bench and was waiting until I felt well enough to return to my lodgings."

He ended this speech with another little bow of his head—which Jemima thought a little overdone. She could not help but return his cheeky smile, despite her father standing between them.

Besides, Captain Rotherham had twisted the truth.

Heaven help her, though, if he had revealed the real location where they had met that morning...

"Well, then," her father spoke slowly, his eyes flickering between the tall young man on one side and his daughter on the other, "as no real harm is done, I am sure this can be forgotten."

"I thank you for your understanding, sir," said Captain Rotherham eagerly. "I really do not know what I would have done without Miss Fitzroy's help."

"It was the least I could do," said Jemima quickly.

She had not looked at her father, conscious of the jacket around her, but evidently, her father was no fool.

"So glad my daughter could be of some assistance, Captain Rotherham," he said smoothly. "Captain Hugh Rotherham, did you say?"

Captain Rotherham stared, bemused, and Jemima's embarrassment returned threefold. "Why, yes, sir."

Jemima sighed as she watched her father take in all of what he would consider to be useful information. She could almost hear in her mind what he was thinking.

Handsome man, perhaps too handsome for Jemima, who had not managed to capture the eye or inclination of any gentleman to whom she had previously been introduced. A soldier, that much was apparent; had Jemima made any awkward or offensive comments about the war in France? Must remember to ask her that later. Let us hope she did not make a fool of herself by falling on this poor unfortunate man.

It was all so predictable. Jemima tried not to blush for her father, but did he have to look at Hugh—at the captain with such an obvious hope to make him a son-in-law?

"Capital," Arthur Fitzroy said suddenly. "Excellent."

"It is?" Captain Rotherham ventured to ask.

Jemima's father nodded. "It is. And now if you will excuse us, Captain Rotherham, my daughter and I must return home—but I hope that we shall see you at Miss Caroline Fitzroy and Dr. Stuart Walsingham's engagement party two weeks from now?"

Captain Rotherham's face showed nothing but confusion. "I regret to say I do not know the gentleman and have not been invited," he said honestly.

"Nonsense," said her father with a broad grin. "Consider yourself invited."

CHAPTER FIVE

I T HAD TAKEN Jemima a full week to completely comprehend what had occurred. It seemed too marvelous, too ridiculous, and at the same time, utterly fantastical that she should fall quite literally into the arms of a stranger, and that stranger to be so...fascinating.

And what's more, fascinated with her.

Jemima sank back against her seat at the breakfast table and sighed. Her father had certainly embarrassed them both enough to ensure Captain Rotherham would not be attending Caroline and Dr. Walsingham's engagement ball, for she had nothing but his name to identify him.

Even if she had wished to find him again, there was no way of doing it.

Not that she had been able to stop wild ideas from running through her mind. Ideas that included bumping into him again on the street. Or Hugh—Captain Rotherham—appearing at the door, asking for her. Creeping into her bedchamber in the dead of night...

It had all been too good to be true, Jemima thought to herself, and was unlikely to be repeated. And anyway, shouldn't she be putting such a man—a soldier!—out of her mind?

That morning at breakfast she had volunteered herself to her sisters, as she was going to the center of London to pick up a pair of gloves. They had gone in to be mended, and she was now in dire need of them due to the impending engagement ball.

Jemima had, foolishly, not expected the flurry of desperate requests from her sisters, but she had written them all down dutifully.

"I would go myself, except—"

"Lord, if you could save me the trip—"

"You'll have enough time, won't you?"

It was only now she looked down at the piece of paper that Jemima realized she had just promised away the majority of her day.

Yet, with five sisters, it so often was. She did at least care about her sisters.

They were Fitzroys. They stood together, no matter what occurred.

She retired upstairs just long enough to gather up her reticule and her pelisse, as she would certainly need to protect herself and her cardinal red gown from the raging wind that had blown through London all morning.

Before the eleventh bell had been chimed by the parlor clock, she was out into the streets of London once more.

It took over an hour to locate the perfumery Arabella had insisted she visit.

Two more stops were required to ensure Esther and Lucy's shoes were adequately re-soled in preparation for the countless dances they anticipated in Bath. Strict instructions had been left that their dancing shoes were to be sent on after them, for their patience had worn out, and they had left for Bath without them.

Jemima thought about her sisters wistfully as she waited in the short queue in the cobblers. Bath. She had never enjoyed a Season there. Her father was one of three brothers, and the middle son lived in Bath.

To be in such a place all year round! Jemima had heard her cousins complain about visiting London, which she supposed was only fair, but there was so much to enjoy and see in Bath that one never saw here.

A short venture into a patisserie—all the rage in London, despite the war in France that raged mere hundreds of miles away—meant that by the stroke of one by the church clocks, Jemima had completed the one task given to her by Sophia.

By now, the hem of her gown was brown and sticky with mud and other unidentified things she had accidentally trodden on during her journeys. It was not a particularly favorite gown, but Jemima could already imagine the look of quiet disappointment that would sweep over her stepmother's face when she returned home.

Someone knocked Jemima's elbow so hard, she accidentally dropped all the bundles that she was carrying, save one, straight into the road.

"God above!" Jemima cried, forgetting she was not in the private confines of her family. "Is being careful a commodity now, to only be purchased by those who consider it a basis of civility?"

She swung round to face the person who had caused her to drop the majority of her day's toil into the mud, just as a gentleman said, "I apologize most profusely, I really do—"

The gentleman stopped speaking just as Jemima's mouth fell open.

"Captain Rotherham," she said weakly.

It couldn't be him, Jemima thought wildly. It must be a trick of the light or a man that looks very similar to him.

But no; she saw, with a wrench in her stomach that felt like happiness though she was not entirely sure, that it was indeed him who had unceremoniously fallen on her the week before.

"Miss Fitzroy," Captain Hugh Rotherham said, his voice strange and full of apology.

He was wearing his uniform once more, but he had managed to get the mud and water stains from their first encounter out most admirably—a trait no doubt, thought Jemima, learned on the battlefield.

His hair was still just as wild, and Jemima smiled just to see him before her.

Here he was, in the flesh, no figment of her imagination at all.

But Captain Rotherham was still speaking, and she attended more closely: "I am so heartily sorry for my mistake, you must forgive me—"

"No, no!" said Jemima hurriedly, seeing at a glance that Captain Rotherham's crutch had come loose under his arm, which was surely the reason for the nudge on her elbow. "I did not mean to be so rude—well, I suppose I did but had I known that it was you—"

Captain Rotherham was barely heeding her words; instead, he was leaning down as far as he was able, desperately trying to rescue her parcels from the street before they were run over by a passing carriage.

A pang hit Jemima's stomach when she saw that it was completely impossible for him to reach them, his leg preventing him from aiding her.

A family of four was shepherded away by the father, muttering something under his breath that Jemima would never believe could come from a person's mouth, and one elderly woman paused and pushed a coin into his gloved hand.

Jemima could not help but laugh at the stunned and slightly confused expression on the captain's face.

"She gave me a shilling," he said, completely bewildered. "Why would she do that?"

IT HAD NOT been a good day for Captain Rotherham.

He had been kept up half the night. At first, he had believed it was something that he ate, though he had assumed nothing could disquiet his stomach after the disgusting fare they had been given when in France, when the battle lines were close, when there

49

were but moments to stuff as much sustenance down their throats as possible.

Yet it had not been his stomach. It had been his heart, twisting the more he thought of Miss Fitzroy. Jemima.

The sun had come up, and Rotherham had barely closed his eyes for more than a moment. He was to gain no sleep that night—which in some ways was a blessing.

Although his nightmares had dissipated this last week, the threat of them was always hovering over his pillow.

The crisp morning was full of the blustery wind he had already begun to associate with the London winter. The birdsong revived him, and he strode out toward his favorite park: Hyde Park.

It was not, Captain Rotherham tried to convince himself, because of his encounter with Jemima, he must remember to call her Miss Fitzroy, even in his head—that Hyde Park was his favorite.

To be sure, he had not visited it much before meeting her, but the fact he had found himself there every day in the last week was surely a mere coincidence. Instead of waiting around at their billeted lodgings that had been assigned to them during the winter, that is where he spent his hours.

Captain Rotherham nodded to a gentleman striding through the park, then realized that he had no memory of how he had got there. His thoughts had been so entwined with Jemima that his legs and crutch had taken him, unbidden, to the very bench where they had sat.

If he closed his eyes, he could almost imagine that she was here with him, those serious eyes regarding him as he opened his soul to her.

Dear God, he wished he had touched her more than a handshake in that moment. Before her father had arrived, of course.

What he would have given to feel the softness of her skin, to sense her warmth, to breathe in that fragrance only a woman seemed to have.

Jemima Fitzroy. He could not help but smile whenever he thought of her name. The boisterous, wild, untamed woman who had absolutely no concern with speaking her mind.

Dear God, she bewitched him.

He had certainly told her more than anyone else about his time in France. Even his mother had not been able to pry so much detail from him—yet there was something about Jemima. Something that made it impossible not to speak; something that made him warm, and desperate to bring her closer to him, to feel her skin underneath his fingers, to feel her breath on his...

Captain Rotherham coughed. This was getting him nowhere. It had been a week, a full seven days since he had met her, and what had he done in the meantime?

Had he inquired after her family, discovered her place of abode? Had he written her a letter, called upon her—or even given attending the engagement ball of her sister any real thought?

In any case, he was not entirely sure what reception would greet him, even if he did. Her revulsion for war and anything related to it was a challenge to any further acquaintance. At times he thought he could see something in her eyes that looked like desire, but she confounded him at every turn.

The wind blew autumn leaves toward him, and he shivered. No. He had done nothing to find her. It was too much to expect Jemima to have even the smallest interest in him. She had probably forgotten him already, just another soldier stumbling around London with more injuries than sense.

It was when he was on his way back to his rooms at the Rose and Crown that his crutch had slipped on some wet leaves, causing him to knock the elbow of the elegant woman in front of him.

Shame and embarrassment coursed through him, but Captain Rotherham had truly believed his eyes to be deceiving him when he saw it was Jemima Fitzroy berating him once again.

The coldness of the shilling in his hand brought him back to the present. Jemima was bending down to retrieve her s parcels. He needed to concentrate. Needed to ensure he did not pull her into his arms and taste those pink lips. Needed to prevent himself from giving her a taste of what pleasure he could surely give her if she would only let him.

SHIFTING THE PARCELS wrapped in brown paper in her arms so she had a better grip, Jemima saw with relief that none were grievously harmed in their adventure, and the one package that she had been able to hold onto was Sophia's cakes. She would never have heard the end of it if they had been damaged.

Captain Rotherham was gazing at her with a strange expression. If Jemima did not know better, she would say that something like warmth was pouring out of them, and she felt once again that she was falling into them.

What were the chances?

Jemima coughed. "No harm done, Captain Rotherham, you need not trouble yourself."

"You must allow me to apologize, at least," said Captain Rotherham frankly, moving forward and taking two of the bundles from her arms under one of his.

Jemima gave them up wordlessly, barely taking in that they were once again standing in the middle of the pavement, obstructing all others.

"I shall allow it," she said. "But only if you walk with me."

He hesitated.

Jemima thought in a panic she had been too forward, asked too much of him. After all, she scolded herself, he was a captain in the British army! He probably had countless errands on official business, and he did not have time to dilly dally with—

"It would be my pleasure," Captain Rotherham said gently. "But only," he added, "if we both agree to swear off one particular topic completely."

Jemima raised an eyebrow. "Afraid you'll be out-argued?"

With a shake of his head, Captain Rotherham smiled. "No such thing—but I am so much more than what I have done for the last few years, just as I am sure you are far more than just a beautiful face. I would have you know that man also."

Jemima smiled tentatively, a smile that broadened when it was returned.

This was not the sort of thing that happened to Jemima Fitzroy! This was wild; it was incredible; it was just not possible.

Yet Captain Rotherham seemed genuinely interested in her company. In her body.

No, that was not right. Jemima pushed the thought aside, conscious that he was still standing right before her. She must not make herself foolish. Once Hugh met any of her sisters, if he did attend the engagement ball, he would surely become enamored with another Fitzroy. Arabella, maybe. Esther, certainly.

Shifting her weight so as to balance her precious charges, Jemima said, slightly breathlessly, "Which direction are you headed, Captain Rotherham?"

He shrugged nonchalantly. "Whichever way you are."

Jemima had grown up in London, knew all the streets by heart. She was only but five minutes' walk from home, far too short a distance to have with Captain Rotherham.

She would take a long cut.

"This way then," she said, gesturing to her left.

He fell in beside her, still clutching her bundles tied with string.

As they moved through London, Jemima was acutely aware of the small distance between them. At times it was only two or three inches, at others, her pelisse brushed up against his coat.

She had taken off her gloves in the last shop, and had decided not to put them on again—a decision she was now reveling in. Being so close to him, able to feel the coarseness of his coat as the back of her hand grazed past him...it made Jemima forget where she was going, as she longed for the excuse to rid herself of all her sisters' parcels and take his arm, to take his hand…

Captain Rotherham coughed. "You have certainly been on a fine shopping expedition, Miss Fitzroy! Are all of these in preparation for your sister's engagement ball?"

Jemima laughed and was pushed aside slightly by a pedestrian approaching from the opposite direction. Her arm grazed Captain Rotherham's.

"In a way, yes," she admitted, "though I deny the suggestion they are all mine!"

He returned her laughter. "Yes, it would indeed be fantastic! Are some of these for your sister—what did Mr. Fitzroy say…Caroline?"

Jemima's smile immediately disappeared, a strange pang twisting her stomach. How long had that taken? Two minutes, even less?

Now that they were on the topic of her sisters, she had lost him completely. Arabella or Esther would scoop him up, and she would only see him when he came to call for them.

"Miss Fitzroy?"

Realizing to her embarrassment she had been silent for far too long to be considered civil, Jemima said quickly as she directed them down a left-hand road, "I have five sisters, Captain Rotherham, and so any shopping expedition undertaken by one tends to be excessive."

His eyes widened. "Five sisters! And here I thought that I was hard-done-by with two!"

Jemima laughed. "It is certainly a busy household, I will admit—but we are a…a complicated family."

Captain Rotherham waited for her to continue. When she did not, he said, "I am all ears, Miss Fitzroy."

Jemima tried to ignore the shiver that moved up her spine as he spoke her name. Three syllables should not have such an effect, should they? "My mother died when I was born, and three years later, my papa met Mrs. Selina Forrest—a widow."

"Ah," he said, filling the silence. "She also knew the pain of losing someone precious."

His words surprised her. She had never considered Selina to have lost someone precious, as her papa had done, but of course, she had.

Jemima smiled. "My stepmother also knew the difficulty of raising a daughter alone. She had two of her own. Caroline is the same age as I—you'll be attending her engagement ball—and Esther, who is presently staying with our relatives in Bath. My papa and stepmother have since had three daughters of their own, bringing our family number to eight."

"And yet none of your sisters are blood?"

Jemima shook her head. "Well, Arabella, Lucy, and Sophia, we share the same papa. The whole lot of them have beautiful red and golden hair...and then there's me."

"Hmm," he said thoughtfully. They continued on down the street for a full minute in silence before he added, "It sounds a rather lonely place for you, even with all of those women. All those Fitzroys."

"That's not all of us," she said wryly. "My father has two older brothers, you see. The eldest, William, has Chalcroft, the family estate, and the middle brother Rupert resides in Bath. All three brothers have daughters, and though each has different residences, social circles, and experiences, I believe each prides himself on having the best of them all."

Captain Rotherham laughed. "Men are so easily understood by women, are they not?"

Jemima stepped over a puddle and joined with his laughter. Something strange rippled through her as they shared the moment. Was this what it was like, then, to flirt with a gentleman? To feel akin to him, to feel a sensation of belonging?

"Uncle William has never understood why his brothers ever wanted to leave Chalcroft where they had grown up. Uncle Rupert has never understood why his brothers never wished to settle in the fashionable Bath. And I think my papa has never understood why his brothers ignore London, the glorious capital, where everything and everyone can be found."

"And here you are, such a rare flower," said Captain Rotherham seriously. Jemima shot a look at him out of the corner of her eye but said nothing. "How many Fitzroy cousins are there, then?"

"Twelve in all."

"Yet you are still so lonely."

"How…" she spluttered. It was unfathomable, how he saw right through her. "How on God's green earth did you—"

"I know the signs. My parents were fortunate in having me young in their marriage, but then no other children appeared until sixteen years later."

Jemima's eyes widened. "Sixteen years!"

"Indeed," said Captain Rotherham. "Edith is sixteen years my junior, and Charlotte eighteen years. In fact, we celebrate her seventh birthday in a week."

Jemima twisted her body around to avoid a young man who was pushing past people. "You must have been a lonely child."

"Lonely, yes," he said cheerfully, "but I think that I became lonelier once the girls were born. I was sixteen, ready to start out on my life as a man—but as soon as I was ready and old enough to start to receive the wisdom and advice of my father, he was fully engaged with a baby and then another."

Jemima stared up at him. Captain Rotherham looked forward, just as he had done in the march the day before, a determined look in his eyes, as if by setting his gaze straight ahead he could ignore the pain from the past.

"And so," she said hesitantly, knowing that they had agreed to avoid the subject completely, but unable to prevent herself, "you joined the army?"

Captain Rotherham nodded. He said nothing more for a few minutes, and Jemima let him stay in his silence until he was comfortable. They continued down the street, the hawkers yelling their wares, a few urchins looking decidedly as though they would wish for some of Jemima's parcels.

"The army became a new family. I felt I had no home with my parents, so I sought to create a home for myself with the militia, and that decision has brought me more pride and misery than I could have ever imagined."

Jemima swallowed. This was not the idea of the army she had envisaged. "I have never thought of the army as a family."

He laughed, giving her an excuse to look up at him. It was remarkable, walking down the streets of London with him. Hugh—Captain Rotherham—gained the approving eye of all ladies they passed, yet his attention had not wavered from her.

"No, I guess you wouldn't," he said drily. "But there is much about being part of the military simply impossible to explain. Believe it or not, Miss Fitzroy, there are many within the ranks themselves who think much as you do—though with even less ability to do anything about it."

This was incomprehensible to Jemima. There were men in the army who believed war was wrong, too?

But her thoughts faded as she saw Captain Rotherham's face, for there was pain there, and a sadness that shocked her.

Jemima willed herself to try to bring him out of this dark stupor. "If you think that is misery, try living in my house on laundry day!"

Captain Rotherham laughed despite himself. "Goodness, I do not wonder you occasionally want to leave the house and throw yourself on unsuspecting soldiers!"

Jemima could not help but chuckle at this. "Captain Rotherham, you forget yourself!"

A gentle push from a throng of shoppers determined to move at great speeds meant she and Captain Rotherham came closer once again.

Slowing, Captain Rotherham watched her as they walked.

"I know that we only met a week or so ago," he said quietly, though just loudly enough for Jemima to hear him over the din of an argument in a shop they were passing, "yet I feel as though I have known you for a long time. I feel as though I shall know you for a very long time."

Falling into his eyes seemed to be an occupational hazard when around him, Jemima thought. If she was not careful, she was going to find her feelings absolutely compromised by Captain Rotherham.

Thankfully for Jemima, he did not seem to be expecting a reply. A right-hand turn necessitated that they wait for a few minutes to cross the road, and Jemima's patience started to fray.

"Ten years ago, this would not have been a problem," she hissed underneath her breath. "Just ten years ago, and now look at it! Carriages everywhere, and carts, and no one attending to the road or to those that may wish to cross—"

She suddenly stopped herself, gazing up at Captain Rotherham, who undoubtedly would find it repulsive and most unladylike that she could be so easily moved to anger.

But he was still standing beside her on her right-hand side, her gloves and another unidentifiable parcel clutched in his right hand and his left on his crutch. He was still smiling at her, a smile that pulled her toward him with some invisible force.

Without saying a word, Captain Rotherham smiled broadly, indicated with a nod of the head toward the road—and stepped out.

Jemima gasped. "No, Captain Rotherham!"

Perhaps he had never been to London before, she thought wildly, and clearly had no understanding of how dangerous the streets were!

Yet, despite his wild recklessness, Jemima stared, astounded, at the scene before her. Captain Rotherham strode out into the road as best he could with his crutch, and the carriages simply stopped before him. He was about six feet across when he realized that Jemima was not with him, and he stopped and turned to look back at her.

"Miss Fitzroy?" he said with the most charming smile on his face. "Will you not join me?"

"Are you mad?" Jemima's voice seethed under her breath as she raced to catch up with him. "Are you attempting to pull me into an early grave, Captain Rotherham, because you are certainly doing a very good job of it!"

Captain Rotherham laughed and inclined his head to those drivers before him. They mirrored the gesture.

"You forget," he said quietly to Jemima, "I am no ordinary man."

Jemima looked at him suspiciously. "Is that so?"

Captain Rotherham nodded. "You must not forget I am a soldier, Miss Fitzroy. I am amazed that you so often do—and do not trouble yourself, please, it pleases me so much. To escape that part of my life is so easy with you, it's like breathing. But for them…"

With this, he looked meaningfully at the drivers on the road.

Suddenly Jemima understood his meaning. That crimson jacket he wore could be seen from hundreds of yards down the road, it was so distinctive. It marked him out as a soldier, and the crutch marked him out as a hero. There was no one who was going to put their carriage careering into a wounded soldier who gained those wounds for king and country.

"You are a very wise man, you know that?" Jemima said with a smile as they reached the pavement on the other side. "Perhaps you abuse your position, have you considered that?"

Captain Rotherham returned her smile. "You are a very astute woman. It would have taken at least three times the explanation for most of your sex to understand that."

Jemima tried as best she could not to blush, but it was impossible.

What was going on? Jemima started to chide herself but could not think exactly what she was doing wrong. *That* she was doing something wrong, she was certain of; wandering the streets with a man she barely knew, of the merest acquaintance possible with her father, who had not even met her stepmother? No, there was something deeply wrong there.

Yet, nothing seemed wrong when she was with Captain Rotherham. She did not have to hide the sarcasm that so often came out of her mouth, and he laughed at her dry humor and did not censure it. There was something incredibly reassuring about the physicality of the man, something that she could not put her finger on. As though his strength was far beyond his body. As though his mind saw her for who she truly was and gloried in it.

Jemima swallowed. She should not think such things. It was not seemly for a young lady.

"Where are we?" Captain Rotherham looked around. "I am not an inhabitant of London, and never have been, but I thought I had a generally good idea of where I was most of the time. Where have you taken us?"

At the word *us,* Jemima blushed slightly. "Just a little way from my home, do not fear."

Captain Rotherham glanced at her quickly. "I am more fearful we are just a little way from your home. I was hoping our walk would be substantially longer."

Jemima looked up at him with a questioning smile, one that showed how doubtful she was that his sentiment was true.

"My, Miss Fitzroy," he said quietly, "it saddens me you do not believe me—that you clearly do not consider yourself worthy company."

Jemima laughed bitterly. "Experience is an excellent teacher, Captain Rotherham, and I have been its pupil for many a year."

They fell into silence as they progressed down the road, then Jemima stopped.

"The quickest way is down this alleyway," she said looking at Captain Rotherham, "and it would certainly prevent us from being buffeted about so much."

"The quickest way?"

Jemima could not help but hear the disappointment in his voice. What did it mean?

Nothing, she told herself sternly. Nothing save that he was being polite, and courteous—as all gentlemen should be. *The last thing you need, my girl, is to see more into this than there is. Do not make a fool of yourself.*

She shrugged—as best she could with so many parcels in her arms. "I do not wish to keep you any longer from the business you are undoubtedly neglecting on my behalf."

Captain Rotherham said nothing, seemingly struggling with deciding on how to respond. Jemima found that she was holding her breath.

And then he sighed. "As you wish, Miss Fitzroy. After you."

Ducking into the alleyway on their left, Jemima was surprised to find it was a lot narrower with two attempting to travel through it. As she most often nipped through it on her own when she was going to be late for an appointment, she had never before had to share it with another. Captain Rotherham's elbow grazed hers, and Jemima tried hard to ignore it—to no avail.

The sound of running could be heard behind them, but before Jemima had the forethought to move either to the left or the right, someone rushed past her and Captain Rotherham. They were running so fast that they were almost a blur, but from the little she could see Jemima could tell that he was in dark clothes, a lady's reticule under his arm that certainly did not belong to him.

His shove had scattered their precious bundles to the ground for a second time, and Captain Rotherham had lost his footing, falling against Jemima and pinning her to the wall.

Her back to the bricks, Jemima's eyes widened as she realized just how close the captain now was. So close. She could feel his heartbeat through his jacket, so fast was it racing.

Crutch fallen to the ground, Captain Rotherham had both hands flat against the wall on either side of her, and he steadied himself but did not move away from her. Jemima took a deep breath to balance herself but was immediately overwhelmed by the intensity of their closeness: the polish of his boots; the linen of his shirt; the musk of a man who had recently been hard at work. It was overpowering.

Being so close to him was almost torture.

Jemima was no fool. She was fully aware of what happened in the marriage bed, yet there was a mystery to it, something she could not completely fathom. But standing there, with Captain Rotherham so close to her, his breath mingling with hers, she started to understand.

Understood the irresistible tug that brought two people together. Understood the desire to touch and be touched. Understood how sometimes it was impossible to ignore, and one's decision to remain aloof simply melted away...

"Captain Rotherham?" Jemima said weakly. It was all she could do to speak his name. "Are you...you quite well?"

"Hugh."

The word came out as a whisper, and Jemima was not entirely sure she had caught it correctly. She raised a hand to steady herself but found instead she placed it on his chest, just below his throat.

"What..." said Jemima, her concentration slipping as she gazed into a pair of eyes she never wished to look away from. "What did you say?"

"Hugh," he repeated in a hoarse voice. The look that he was giving her could only be described, Jemima thought wildly, as passionate. "Call me Hugh."

Jemima flushed slightly, but she knew intuitively what she wanted to do. Raising her chin slightly, she leaned forward and closed the gap between them with her lips on his.

What came over her, she did not know. But she had to have him. Had to know what it was to kiss him, know what it was to be consumed by his touch.

If she had been distracted by him before, it was nothing to how she felt now.

Jemima's kiss was hesitant at the beginning; it was her first, after all, and she was still not entirely sure it was welcome.

Hugh's response, however, soon told her just how welcome it was. His lips gently caressed her own, his left hand moving to her waist. A steadying hand that brought her close, her breasts pushed up against his chest, crutch forgotten.

Jemima had never felt so warm in all her life. All outside surroundings had disappeared, and she could be anywhere. Nothing mattered but Captain Rotherham and his gorgeous mouth.

As he turned his head slightly, she could feel the rough graze of a day's worth of stubble. Leaning into him, Jemima's hands moved to the back of his neck, pulling him closer.

Her mind was filled with him. Hugh. He certainly knew what he was doing, his passionate kisses shooting tingles of pleasure across her body. Jemima moaned, unable to stop herself, but it did not offend him.

Hugh groaned, pulling her closer, gently encouraging her lips apart. Guided by him wordlessly, abandoning herself to the pleasure, Jemima obliged—and almost opened her eyes in shock.

His tongue lightly explored her separated lips, then ventured into the soft warmness of her mouth. Meeting her own, he kissed her passionately with no thought as to time or place.

Jemima clung to him as if he were the last man alive in the world, yet long before she was ready for it to be over, it was.

Hugh lifted his head and opened his eyes. "Jemima," he said, his voice jagged. His eyes were sparkling, despite the darkness of the alleyway.

She gazed up at him, wordless, speechless, thoughtless.

The moment could have remained between them for minutes, but eventually, Hugh's gaze dropped. "Miss Fitzroy," he said in a whisper, "I think I should probably return you home now."

CHAPTER SIX

"**A**ND I JUST can't believe how happy I am!"

Repeat that one more time, Jemima thought, biting her tongue to ensure she would not speak aloud, *and I will make sure that you never bother me again.*

"I am sure you cannot," Jemima said quietly. Caroline was so enwrapped in her thoughts, she did not heed the sarcasm dripping from every syllable as Jemima warned herself silently that her sister's inability to notice would not continue indefinitely.

Caroline sighed as she held up a cream dress with golden embroidery around the hem and the neckline, trying to find somewhere to stand where she could see herself in the looking glass. She was dressed only in her undergarments, angling her body to try and create the illusion that she was wearing the dress. "It was ever so much a surprise, you know."

Jemima didn't say anything, but Caroline did not need her cooperation to continue.

Flinging the dress she was holding onto the floor, she picked up another which had rather more decoration around the sleeves. "I had absolutely no idea he was going to propose marriage. I thought he was merely interested in telling me about his family's chosen portrait artist—but of course, they are waiting to have the portrait painted until we are married you see, so I can be included…"

It was difficult for Jemima to be around her stepsister at the moment, though it did not appear that Caroline had noticed.

The engagement ball was that evening, and Caroline had spent the entire day working herself—and her sisters Arabella and Sophia—into a frenzy of preparation. Sophia had only collapsed into tears twice, which Jemima personally considered rather impressive considering the heightened feelings of the occasion.

As the only one who was not permitted by their parents to attend the engagement ball, Sophia was starting to bear the disappointment well. At least, Jemima had her suspicions that the only reason she had not dissolved into floods of tears as the evening drew near was because of the treats from the patisserie, carried in the arms of a slightly flustered Jemima.

"And then I thought my gloves, they simply would not do! Yet I think on reflection, they will do very well. Don't you think the plans for the reception itself exquisite? I told Walsingham, I said…"

But for Caroline, there was nothing to do but discuss herself—her and Stuart Walsingham's happiness.

Every conversation circled around it or dived straight in. It was impossible to speak to her but hear Dr. Walsingham's name; the more one attempted to avoid it, the more surprising it was when it suddenly appeared.

Even Arabella, the peacemaker of the family, had snapped once or twice when in a seemingly innocent conversation about pianoforte music, Caroline had once again introduced Dr. Walsingham and his far superior musical tastes.

As it was, Jemima kept a vapid smile on her face and her mouth shut as her stepsister wittered on.

"…and his entire family loves me, naturally—well why would they object, and on what grounds? There is not much family left, to be sure, only his mother and his younger sister. But then I am so accustomed to sisters, it really was no trouble at all to…"

Jemima nodded slowly, hoping that was the response Caroline was expecting. She was also in her undergarments but had a robe wrapped around her. Dressing for the engagement ball was not her particular priority.

Her mind was on a far different gentleman, one she had spent a good amount of time dwelling on, in the moments when she could ignore her surroundings.

Only ever able to meet by appointment in the town, she and Hugh had spent the best part of five days over the last week walking together, avoiding the past, talking about the present—and at least in her mind, secretly hoping for the future. It was a dangerous area they avoided speaking of, yet Jemima desperately hoped he would one day speak it.

He would, wouldn't he? After all, it would be most disgraceful if he did not, after stealing so many kisses from her.

Stealing. Jemima tried to keep her expression calm as she thought about it, but her cheeks pinked. She had given them willingly, wished for more, longed for the next moment they would touch.

Jemima smiled as she thought about their meeting that morning, and Hugh's words to her as they fought their way through to Hyde Park.

"I still cannot comprehend why you desire my company," Hugh had admitted in a slightly embarrassed tone. "Not when you were so prejudiced against the uniform that I wear."

And Jemima had replied: "Is it so strange?"

They had met by chance, then by design, then by frantic planning, desperate to see each other without the typical chaperones usually enforced on the young and the—in love?

Jemima's cheeks heated, and a clatter in the room brought her rapidly to the present.

Caroline was rummaging through the chest of gloves and stockings she and Jemima shared. As the two eldest children, they had shared a room for as long as they could remember, yet it was not until now Jemima felt the awkwardness of it.

"You are an engaged woman," she said suddenly.

Caroline halted in her search for the glove to match the one she already had and stared at her stepsister.

"I know," she said quietly. "Isn't it strange?"

Their eyes met. "You have always just been...Caroline. And now you are going to be living elsewhere, and," with a hesitation, "and be Mrs. Walsingham."

Caroline broke into a huge smile and began to laugh with joy. "It's so hard to keep the laughter in! To think, after so long, that Stuart and I—Dr. Walsingham and I, of course," and the silly grin returned to her face, "will be married before spring is here! It really does make you think just how quickly one's fortune can change, doesn't it? I never thought..."

And her chatter returned.

Jemima's smile hid her grimace. She felt as though she was watching everything on a stage at the opera.

In fact, since Hugh had returned her to her door and bid her a hasty farewell, Jemima had found it rather difficult to complain at all.

She was on a cloud much higher whenever her mind turned to Captain Hugh Rotherham.

They had learned quickly which topics to avoid—those too painful, those which would cause an argument, those which she could never be persuaded to agree on. There were times when he mentioned something that made her bristle, yet her growing admiration for him proved to be a better censure than all previously attempted by her family.

"Jemima?"

And her father had invited Hugh to the engagement ball that evening; it was only a few more hours and she would be able to see him again. They had barely been able to stop meeting each other after their ardent alleyway kiss; what would he say to her this evening?

"Jemima!"

With a start, Jemima blinked. Caroline was not five inches away from her face and had a confused expression.

"Jemima, I have been standing here a full minute, trying to gain your attention!" Caroline said, almost scolding. "What on earth has got into your head that you should be so far away?"

"Nothing of consequence," said Jemima automatically. She had learned from a young age that having a household full of women could only mean drama at every opportunity, and removing herself from the occasion benefited them, just as much as it did her.

Caroline gazed at her suspiciously, turned to sit on the side of the bed, and looked up at her stepsister with a questioning look on her face. "You've been quiet, Jemima."

"Quiet?"

"Too quiet," returned Caroline. "This is not like you."

Jemima rose and wandered across to the large bay window in their shared bedroom, dropping down onto the floor and the cushion she had placed there, gazing out into London.

She did not reply, but once again Caroline did not require her to participate in the conversation. "Normally you would have snapped at me—or shouted at me—or told me how irksome it was for you, having me talk about Stuart...Dr. Walsingham...continuously. Yet you have not crossed me with a single harsh word all morning!"

Jemima laughed with a calculated nonchalant air. "Is it really so much to think perhaps I am happy for you and have no wish to make you miserable?"

"Well, yes."

Burning with shame, Jemima determinedly did not turn away from the window to look at her stepsister. "It hurts you would assume that of me," she said quietly, watching a chimney sweep move along the street, knocking door to door, obviously hoping for some more business before Christmas.

But although Jemima could not see Caroline's expression, it did not appear to have changed her stepsister's mind. Caroline seemed convinced there was something suspicious going on.

"But—" Caroline began to say, but she was interrupted by the opening of the bedroom door.

Jemima turned her head eagerly, hoping for some news of Hugh—though why he would be sending her news she had absolutely no idea—her eyes lost their sparkle as she saw it was her stepmother who had entered the room.

Selina bustled over to her eldest daughter. "Caroline, if you do not have things nailed down around you, then they will start to go walking away. Here," and she held out the matching glove to the one in Caroline's hands, "I found this."

Caroline's raptures were unabashed by her mother's gentle dig at her tidiness. "Thank you, Mama," she beamed. "I do not know what I would have done without you—Jemima and I were frantic with worry, we had no idea where else to look!"

"Jemima?" Selina said in a confused tone. Caroline pointed to the window, and Selina turned her neck to look. "Jemima! I had not seen you there, I do beg your pardon."

"Think nothing of it, Mama," was Jemima's reply.

She had spoken almost without thinking, her eyes absorbed by the progress of the chimney sweep and her mind absorbed by Hugh. It was not until the words were out of her mouth that she sighed inwardly. Such a polite response was sure to elicit more confusion than a rude one would have.

"My word, Jemima, what has got into you?"

"I was about to tell you," said Caroline eagerly, standing up from the bed and taking her mother's arm as she spoke. "I do not believe that Jemima is entirely well, Mother. She has not been herself for the last day or two, and in the last hour she has behaved in a most peculiar manner."

Jemima sighed, then spoke despite knowing she would not be heeded. "I am quite well, I assure you."

"Unwell!" Selina narrowed her eyes as she examined her. "You certainly do sound out of sorts, Jemima. Have you eaten anything which you believe may have disagreed with you?"

A million retorts, each one ruder than the last, would have sprung up in her mind at any other occasion, but Jemima's mind was not really even in the room. She was already imagining Hugh's entrance at the engagement ball, taking his arm, dancing every dance with him, ignoring the rest of the world.

When her stepmother spoke again, Jemima started, not realizing Selina had moved closer and closer to her as she had been lost in her thoughts.

"You do not look sickly," said Selina thoughtfully, putting the back of her hand to Jemima's forehead.

"I am one and twenty years old, not a child!"

"You are a little warm, but nothing of any consequence, nothing that would concern me enough to fetch a doctor—unless you wish me to, Jemima?"

Brushing away Selina's hand with her own, Jemima muttered, "I am quite well."

Caroline had not crossed the room with her mother but had sunk back onto the bed—and a glint in her engagement ring which caught her eye made her smile mischievously.

"Perhaps Mama," she said, her smile broadening, "Jemima *is* sick, but we do not know the exact cause yet—but will tonight!"

Both Selina and Jemima turned their heads to look at Caroline at these words, confusion painted on both their faces.

"Tonight?" Selina asked, confusion turning into bewilderment. "What is happening tonight?"

Caroline giggled and said, "Perhaps Jemima is *lovesick*. Perhaps her cure will be attending my engagement ball this very evening!"

Both she and her mother laughed as Jemima's cheeks burned. She willed them to stay pale and cool, but it seemed that she had lost all her faculties, including her ability to control her expression.

Her clear discomfort only made Caroline laugh harder.

"Who is he, your young man follower?" She said gleefully. "Butcher, baker, or candlestick maker?"

"Now, now then," said Selina, having gained control of her laughter, "there is no reason to tease your sister."

"There is plenty of reason to tease my sister!"

"No one," Jemima muttered, rising from the floor and moving over to the table where the jewelry she and Caroline were going to wear that evening had been laid out. "There is no one that—"

"Tinker, tailor, soldier, sailor, rich man, poor man, beggar man, thief?" Caroline sang, tipping her head from side to side with each word.

At that moment, Jemima hated her sister, hated her stepmother, hated that she had ever got herself in this mess.

Of course Captain Hugh's attendance at her sister's engagement ball could not possibly be simple! Of course her family would find some way of ridiculing her; the idea a man could ever be a part of her existence was subject for mirth enough.

"Interesting you should say that, my dear," said Selina thoughtfully. "Your papa did mention inviting a young man of Jemima's acquaintance. A soldier, was he not?"

That was the final straw. If she had not been teased beyond endurance over the years, if she had not been sidelined again and again for Caroline's beauty, or Arabella's elegance, or even little Sophia's brains, perhaps Jemima would not have reacted so.

As it was...

"What business is it of yours? Are you so desperate to marry me off, to get rid of me that you would force me toward any gentleman that I happen to converse with? I refuse to marry just to please you, and if that means that I end up an old spinster with no one to love me or care for me, then so be it!"

Caroline and Selina's mouths were open wide, but they had no chance to reply as Jemima had already stormed from the bedchamber.

CHAPTER SEVEN

"**S**PECTACULAR DRESS, IN my opinion."

"Oh yes, the cream satin? Not a very unique design, of course, but carried off so well."

"Caroline Fitzroy can carry off cream so well, it's her coloring, of course."

"That hair! I was amazed at how simple she kept it. I saw Miss Marnion try something very outlandish for her engagement ball last month, however, and it was quite a failure, we all agreed. Perhaps Miss Fitzroy is keeping her hair simple and elegant for that very reason."

"You could be quite right, my dear, quite right."

The two matronly women who were speaking were resting their feet and sitting on two gold gilt chairs at the edge of the dancing. The entire ballroom in the Fitzroy house had been decorated with the Christmas colors of red and burnished gold, reminding everywhere anyone looked of Caroline Fitzroy's beautiful hair.

"And the food is quite excellent."

"Indeed, and the punch plentiful! These are essential assets to a ball, very few young ladies these days think of such things."

"Ah," said one of the women knowledgeably, "but it would have been Mrs. Selina Fitzroy who has organized the details, surely?"

"Indeed," her friend nodded. "And I am glad she has chosen those musicians." She nodded toward the collection of six musicians sitting opposite them, playing for the ten or so couples that were dancing in the center of the room. "They are enthusiastic, the finest quality. I have heard tell of a mere flute ensemble for some balls, if you can credit it."

"My favorite thing so far," confided the first woman, "is that Dr. Walsingham has so far asked young Miss Fitzroy to dance every single dance with him—and she accepted!"

Her companion beamed. "Yes, their love is palpable, though Miss Fitzroy is fortunate, evidently from a very loving family."

Six seats down from the two gossiping women, Jemima sat and attempted not to eavesdrop.

Despite the noise from the musicians and the shouting and whooping from the dancers, she could hear every word they were saying most clearly. She was not entirely sure whether she should be listening, but then they were in her home. Surely, she may listen to whatever she liked.

"Ah, the Fitzroys," sighed the woman, wriggling her feet so as to ease her slippers off. "Such a hospitable family. Did you see every one of her sisters danced at least twice so far? Such an obliging family."

"Not so," her friend said triumphantly. "Miss Jemima has not danced at all!"

Jemima shrank back in her seat and willed their eyes to pass over her as they swept round, making sure no one from the family was close enough to hear.

"Most strange," was the reply from the woman without her slippers on. "At her own sister's engagement party? Is she so particular she could not find a gentleman to stand up with her?"

"Stepsister," corrected her companion, pulling out her fan and wafting it over herself in an attempt to cool down.

"Stepsister? Oh, of course. Sometimes I forget just how complicated the Fitzroy family really is."

The candles were starting to reach their last, and many of the guests had started to think about calling their carriages, now eleven o'clock had just rung out across London.

Jemima wished silently that the two women, who clearly had nothing better to do than to comment on her dancing, or lack thereof, would leave, but they appeared to be in no hurry to return to their homes.

She could not believe it. She had really convinced herself Hugh would attend the ball, had really thought he would wish to see her, more formally at last.

After all their conversation, all those kisses...her cheeks reddened slightly. It had all been leading to something, at least that was what she had thought. She had believed Hugh would wish to court her, to dance with her, to see her with her family.

Even despite all the teasing she had endured from Caroline, she had longed to see him. Yet Jemima had spent the entire ball waiting for something to occur that never did.

She had even put a modicum of thought into her attire, not something she had been wont to do before.

Her satin dress rather stood out beautifully when it was lying on her bed, but here in the evening it was Caroline, of course, that glowed—yet Jemima had purposefully chosen sapphire ear bobs to match, her black slippers had been embroidered delicately with sapphire thread. Even her hair contained a sapphire ribbon pinned up by the lady's maid she shared with Caroline.

And yet despite all of that effort and thought and concern over her appearance, Hugh had not come to the engagement ball.

Jemima had waited downstairs half an hour before guests were invited to arrive, eager for his arrival. As guest after guest arrived, she had looked past them, sure the next person would be Hugh.

She had spent just over three hours waiting for him.

She had greeted people and bore the indignity of her father standing behind her, as though checking at every moment that she was acting with proper decorum.

And he had not come. And now the ball was almost over,

thought Jemima dully.

It was foolish of her to raise her hopes up so high. She should have caught herself from making such a mistake. But then, she countered silently, she had never had such a close attachment to a gentleman before in all her life.

No man had ever looked at her the way that Hugh did; no man had ever spoken to her like Hugh had; certainly, no man had ever kissed her in the manner that Hugh did in that dark alleyway, away from the world.

A shiver made her smile, but it was short-lived. What had those kisses meant if Hugh did not wish to attend her family ball? Was there any earnestness in his attentions, or was this all just a flirtation for him? She knew so little about soldiers, after all.

Obviously, Captain Hugh Rotherham had not considered the engagement party worth attending.

Not that any of her family had noticed her misery, Jemima thought bitterly. Her father had seemingly forgotten that he had even invited someone on her behalf, and her stepmother lost all notion of the rest of her family as soon as Caroline had walked into the ballroom.

Jemima had to admit her sister did look beautiful. The cream satin gown and tiny diamond bob earrings complemented her red hair perfectly.

Sadness overwhelmed her, weighing her heavily against the chair. Hugh had certainly been worth caring about—yet her feelings were clearly not reciprocated.

Jemima heard a bubble of laughter and raised her eyes to see Caroline whirl about in the dance. Caroline had forgotten her teasing of earlier, had seemingly forgotten the rest of the world existed now she was dancing in the arms of Dr. Walsingham.

Any other time, the offense of being ignored so publicly would have rubbed against Jemima's temper; but not this evening. This evening, Jemima was a little heart sore.

"Miss Fitzroy?"

Jemima blinked. She knew that voice...

Standing just to her left, previously out of her view thanks to a gaggle of elderly gentlemen with smoking pipes, was a tall man with wild, jet-black hair, seemingly untamable. He had dark sparkling eyes and wore his best regimental uniform, topped with a scarlet jacket. The crutch on his left side was steady, yet his face seemed unsure of the reception he was about to receive.

And well he might be.

"You finally decided to attend, did you?" Jemima said, pain in every syllable, unable to keep the hurt from her voice. "After everything that has—that we—you would think you could orchestrate arriving on time!"

Her words had caught the attention of the two matronly women sitting to her right, and one of them peered up at the gentleman facing Miss Jemima's ire.

Hugh smiled nervously, all of his usual confidence gone. "Your family has a wonderful home here, Jemima, and—"

"Home, home, is that what you wish to talk about?" Jemima heard her words as if they were a long way off. She knew what she was saying was cruel, yet she could not seem able to stop herself, so great was her disappointment.

Hugh's smile disappeared, and his eyes darkened. "I knew that you would be angry, Jemima, but—"

"Do not call me that!" she hissed. "And keep your voice down. I do not wish you to become acquainted with my family. After this evening, we shall not see each other again."

Rising angrily, Jemima made to walk away from him, but Hugh grabbed her arm.

"Jemima." His voice was soft and pleading, and the simplest touch had Jemima pause.

Her lips ached for him in a way that she had not known was possible. It was not the only part of her that ached. She longed for him, longed for his touch. Seeing him here, in Society, was agony.

She swallowed but kept her face staring at the dancers, refusing to look at him.

"Jemima, you must permit me to explain."

"What can you possibly say to undo the hurt you have caused me, Captain Rotherham?" Jemima said quietly, finally turning her eyes to his.

It was fortunate for Jemima she had not taken more than one step before Hugh spoke again, or it was likely she would not have been able to hear him, his words were so soft.

"I was afraid."

Jemima turned to gaze at the soldier who had fought wars, who had seen battles, and had lived longer than many men in that same world.

"Afraid?"

"I…" For the first time since Jemima had known him, Hugh actually looked visibly uncomfortable. He opened his mouth a second time, but nothing came out.

Jemima unconsciously moved closer to him and took his right hand with her left. She said nothing, but the look in her eyes encouraged him to go on.

"I have never been to a ball or a dance since…well, since my injury in France."

Compassion flowed through her veins and softened her heart. Within moments, Jemima felt nothing but shame.

HUGH WATCHED HER expression change as his very soul twisted. What kind of man was he to bring this woman into his life, to bring her closer to him? What could he offer her? Him, a man who could not even gain the courage to attend a ball—an engagement ball, no less, when the discourtesy would not only be given to Jemima but also to her sister, her intended, their father…

He had spent over an hour pacing uncomfortably up and down the room that he shared with the other men from the regiment. The sound of his crutch hitting the wooden floor felt harsh in his ears, and he struggled to resist the temptation to loosen his collar.

"I see no problem," the colonel said frankly. "She is a woman who likes you, you are a man who likes her—I cannot conceive the impediment!"

Hugh snorted. "Even you must comprehend why my attendance at a ball—a celebration of a marriage, in which there will be copious dances—is completely impossible."

"You have an injured leg." The colonel's voice was matter of fact and drew a slightly embarrassed tinge in Hugh's face. "You are not the first, and you will, sadly, not be the last. It is time to face up to the reality that unless God sees fit, this is how you will be for the rest of your life."

Hugh did not respond to this, no matter how reasonable it was.

He was not looking for reasonable discussions, not today. He had paced up and down, his leg aching from the exertion, in his best dress uniform, yet could not bring himself to go.

He would not shame her. He would not shame himself.

"After all," said the colonel quietly, "from the small amount that you have told me, the lady does not appear to be concerned with the crutch at all. Why should she be now? Your biggest concern should not be yourself, but her attitudes toward this war. Does she not realize things are getting worse? Cannot she understand that eventually, we could be sent back there?"

Hugh turned at one end of the room and started back down it again, not meeting the eyes of his companion.

The colonel sighed. "If you are truly not to attend, Rotherham, you had best send a message to the lady now. The engagement ball began half an hour ago, and it will take that time again for a servant to make their way there. She should be told."

Hugh laughed darkly. "And remove myself from her company once and for all? Have her lose all faith in me, so she refuses to see me again? So I never have the blessing of seeing her face again? I agree, perhaps that is the best course."

And it was not merely her face that he wished to see, though he would hardly admit as much to the colonel.

No, it was all of Jemima he wished to see, Hugh thought, his hand clenching into a fist. He had seen much of her soul, but it was her body he wished to ravish now.

To bed her, to show her what pleasure was. To prove to himself he could still bring a woman to such ecstasies she would cry his name and—

"Nonsense."

Hugh's eyes darted over to the colonel.

"If you love this woman," said the colonel with an intense stare, "if there is even a modicum of acquaintanceship with her, then the least you can do is attend her sister's engagement ball. I loved the one I lost, and the only solace I have now is in writing to her parents. If there had been one single moment I could reclaim with her, even if it was under the most uncomfortable of circumstances, I would take it with both hands. Even if I had lost both legs altogether."

A stunned silence followed this. Hugh swallowed.

Then he strode toward the door as best he could with his crutch, flung it open, and walked through it without a backward glance.

It was only now Hugh wondered whether he had acted right, yet Jemima's expression was certainly softening.

"Oh Hugh," Jemima said softly, taking a step closer to him. "Why did you not tell me that—or when Papa invited you in the first place? We would have understood—"

"Would you?" Hugh said bitterly, and he hated himself for the way it made Jemima flinch slightly. "You seemed very quick to assume the worst of me."

"It hurt that you were not here," Jemima said simply, all her anger dissipated. "I had wanted you here so badly, and you were not here, and I thought…"

Hugh's eyebrow raised quizzically, his bitterness gone. "What did you think?"

Jemima swallowed and whispered, "I did not know if my

kisses…whether they pleased you. We have not spoken of them, so I did not know—"

It was all Hugh could do not to sweep her into his arms. Freeing his hand from hers, he raised it to her chin and tilted it up so that she was looking straight into his eyes.

"Hear this, Miss Jemima Fitzroy," he said in a dark tone full of emotion. "If we were not standing in a ballroom surrounded by other people, I would be doing much more than kissing you at this moment."

HEAT RUSHED THROUGH Jemima's body like a wave, and she found herself transfixed by Hugh's mouth.

"If we were not standing in a ballroom surrounded by other people, I would be doing much more than kissing you at this moment."

She had no thought, no conscious decision about what she was going to do: almost of its own accord, her hand clasped his and she started to walk.

"Jem—Miss Fitzroy, where are we going?" Hugh voiced his confusion as Jemima began to hear murmurs around the room. She knew she was attracting the attention of those watching, but there was no going back.

Jemima smiled. "We are going to dance."

"Dance?" Hugh's voice was firm. "We are doing absolutely no such thing. Did you not listen to a word I said? The whole reason—"

"Jemima? Who is your friend?"

Cringing internally at Caroline's falsely interested tone, Jemima ignored the lady of the ball and marched down the set of dancers to the end.

Hugh stopped dead, and there was nothing Jemima could do to move him. "No, I cannot do this."

Jemima smiled at him, all anger and bad temper melted away. Though unsure precisely what it was called, this emotion that flooded her veins whenever she saw him, she knew it was here to stay.

She wanted him. Needed him. And she would prove it to him.

"Hugh," she said quietly, "I understand you were nervous about coming here—and if I had any hint of intelligence in my bones, I would have known that before you told me. But can't you see? I…I'm not embarrassed or nervous of you, and I am not ashamed to be seen with you! In fact," she said, gaining boldness, "I *want* to be seen with you. I want to dance with you, and I want to do it now. Here. Before my family."

There was a strange look on Hugh's face, and suddenly Jemima was unsure of herself. Had she spoken too much, been too abrupt or forward?

She had certainly never spoken to any other gentleman in this way. She had never wished to.

He hesitated, then said softly, "I have never met anyone so blunt as you."

The musicians started up the opening musical phrase that heralded a slow country dance, and she did not look away from him.

"Why not," he said, striding forward as best he could and standing opposite her. "You amaze me, Miss Jemima Fitzroy."

Jemima amazed herself. It was not the first time she had ever danced with a gentleman at a ball, of course—the name Fitzroy alone was enough for most young men to show even a partial interest—but there had been few that had truly asked out of their interest in herself. She was fully aware that many of them had merely crumbled under the gaze of her father.

But this was the first time she had asked a gentleman to dance, and it was Hugh that stood opposite her. The handsome man in a uniform.

Trying to ignore the whispers spreading around the room like wildfire, Jemima looked down the new set to see who was going to be dancing with them. She was unsurprised to see Caroline and

Dr. Walsingham were next to them, and on the other side of them was a slightly older couple she did not recognize.

Arabella and a young man Jemima thought was a Mr. Caversham, although she could be wrong, were further down the set, and a slightly portly and elderly gentleman led a woman in an old-fashioned dress to stand beside Jemima and Hugh.

Jemima smiled at her partner, who gave her a half-smile. Hugh was clearly uncomfortable, but for all of his fears, he stood there, holding his crutch and not taking his eyes away from hers.

Jemima almost stumbled into the woman next to her when the music started. She giggled, unable to help herself, and she heard Hugh's laugh joining hers.

The dance was not fast, which was fortunate for Hugh, but Jemima saw no one considered his crutch a hindrance.

In fact, the dance progressed and got slightly more lively as people threw themselves into the movements. Hugh even became more animated, the smile growing on his face, and he started to join in with the whoops and shouts.

Each time their hands touched, Jemima felt as though the gravity of the world shifted slightly. Heat passed between them, a knowing heat that promised something delicious and forbidden later on that evening.

Jemima attempted to focus on the dance and not wonder whether it would be possible for the two of them to find a moment in a quiet corner. For a man with six daughters, her father had disobligingly made it rather difficult to speak to a gentleman alone.

Not that she planned to do much speaking.

When they drew closer in part of the dance, Hugh said quietly into her ear, "I can't take my eyes off you."

Jemima blushed. "You amaze me, once again. It is so wonderful to see you enjoy yourself."

Their hands touched once more, and Hugh shivered slightly.

Jemima whispered, "You feel it, too?"

The dance was ending, but in an act of daring when they

came together, Hugh placed his arm around her waist. "I feel nothing else."

Jemima opened her mouth, determined to ask him just exactly what he meant by that comment. Surely, he could not say such things without expecting her to question—

But before she could, a scream was emitted by the woman beside her who was dancing with the portly old man. Jemima and Hugh turned to see the man clutching his heart. He staggered but fell to the floor, his face red.

Screams could be heard from around the room, and Jemima could pick out Caroline's in particular. Her stepsister and Dr. Walsingham rushed over to the man.

"Make way, I'm a doctor!"

One of the men who had been dancing pushed past Jemima, who had stepped forward although she didn't know exactly how she would be able to help. Hugh's arm was still around her, and she leaned into him, his strength holding her as nothing else could.

Dr. Walsingham knelt down, loosened the cravat from the man's neck, and reached for his wrist to feel his pulse.

Jemima had never experienced such silence before as the entire party waited to hear Dr. Walsingham's pronouncement— but she did not have to wait long for him to speak.

As soon as Dr. Walsingham dropped the elderly gentleman's wrist down to the floor and stood up with sadness and shock on his face, she knew.

"He is gone."

CHAPTER EIGHT

"GREAT-UNCLE EDWARD!"

Jemima stared at the chaos causing the evening to fall apart before her eyes. Caroline had fallen to the ground beside the gentleman as Dr. Walsingham cradled his head in his lap, clearly distressed.

Arthur Fitzroy was roaring orders to the servants, and Selina was attempting to calm Sophia, who had been permitted to sit and watch the last hour of dancing and was now in tears.

Guests moved around the room in a frenzy, half of them trying to help though they could offer no real assistance or expertise, and the other half gossiping about the catastrophe that was occurring right in front of their eyes.

Dr. Walsingham was still repeating his great-uncle's name. "Uncle Edward, please speak to me…"

Beside him stood Hugh, his complexion pale and waxen. He wasn't swaying exactly, but he was certainly struggling to stand upright. Jemima could see that the fingers around his crutch were white as he clenched it desperately.

"Captain Rotherham—" Jemima clung onto him, unsure what she intended to say but knowing she had to say something. Hugh was pale, paler than she had ever seen before.

Without a word, he released her.

"Hugh?"

Before she could move toward him once more, Hugh had clearly had enough. Ignoring her completely, he marched out of the room onto the garden terrace.

Jemima took one look at Caroline and saw she was ably comforting Dr. Walsingham. A glance around the room saw Arabella now caring for their younger sister Sophia.

And so, Jemima turned on her heels. The garden terrace was her destination, and at that moment, she truly believed nothing but an earthquake or some similar disaster could hold her from it.

"Captain Rotherham?" She said, peering around the corner of the door to the garden terrace. The air was cool here, welcome after the heat of the dancing. "Hugh?"

He was standing on the balcony, looking out at the moon. It was full and sat heavy in the sky, without any clouds to hinder its light.

"It's the same moon, you know," he said softly.

Jemima stepped lightly over to him and impulsively placed her hand over his right, placed for balance on the balcony.

"It's always the same moon."

Hugh did not look at her, did not smile—but he did not move his hand away. His expression seemed pained, and Jemima wanted nothing more than to help him, to care for him—perhaps, even to love him.

Love. She should not think such a thing. Not until he had spoken first, and this was not the moment.

"I used to think when I was in France or wherever else Napoleon forced us to be, that when I looked up at the moon, it was the same moon," said Hugh quietly. "No matter where I was, I would always be able to look up at the sky and see the same moon. When my parents looked up at the night sky, the light that fell on them would be the same moonlight that fell on me, wherever I was."

Jemima's heart ached for him and his pain, his loneliness. It was loneliness she now realized, she could fully comprehend.

"It's the same moon," she said in barely a whisper.

Hugh shifted his hand so he could squeeze hers. Then he brought it to his chest and held it over his heart.

"I..." He tried to speak, but he didn't seem to have the words. Jemima waited a moment, then he began again. "I must apologize to your family when we return. Was not that gentleman a member of your family?"

Jemima shook her head slightly. "A relation of Dr. Walsingham, as far as I am aware."

"Still, you have a family connection to the man," said Hugh angrily, "and all I could do was stand there. A soldier should know better!"

"A soldier does know better," said Jemima forcefully. She pulled on her hand so Hugh was forced to face her. "You have seen more of sickness and death than everyone else in that room combined! It is no wonder that, at the fresh sight of it, you were hesitant to embrace it!"

"There goes the pacifist," said Hugh in a low mocking tone, but a smile danced across his cheeks. "I am glad, believe me, that you can have such ideals. The chance to hold such things are not afforded to all, and any knowledge you can be spared is a gift that is my pleasure to bestow upon you."

"Meeting you...knowing you have opened my eyes," admitted Jemima quietly. "I look back on all my opinions now with a little surprise. How could I hold such passionate thoughts without fully knowing what I spoke?"

Hugh gazed at her intently. "I wish I could make you understand," he said quietly, "I wish I could even comprehend it myself, the way that I have changed. Not just my leg, of course." A wry smile followed this statement. "I mean in myself. In my character, in the way I view the world, the way I think. I know scars of the body will eventually fade, and I shall never win any races, but my leg will probably heal. Yet the scars of the mind I do not think shall ever fully mend."

Jemima's hand was still trapped by Hugh's, held close to his chest. If she concentrated, she could feel his heartbeat.

It was so different, being here with him in the darkness of night. Their conversation felt more secret, their privacy for once assured rather than hoped for. Hugh's gaze was transfixed on her face. The moonlight fell softly onto his features as if it caressed him.

"I do not think," she said in a whisper, "you will have to bear them as you do now, even if their complete healing is something to long for but not to expect. With time, you will grow to carry them as badges of honor. As proof that you have done something courageous."

Her eyes found Hugh's. Jemima saw to her surprise that she could see the stars reflected in them, their depth given new character and meaning as she sank into them.

Impulse, pure and simple impulse, was the only thing driving Jemima now.

Reaching up her free hand, she placed her arm around him, and bringing her body close to his, she hugged Hugh in a deep embrace.

Her wish to comfort him, however, soon transformed into something much more primal. Her desire for him could be hidden no longer, and it was no secret that he wanted her, too.

His hand released his crutch, which fell to the ground with a clatter—a clatter that sounded a long way off. Jemima's face was buried in Captain Rotherham's shoulder, and at first glance, anyone who ventured out onto the garden terrace would have assumed that their embrace was nothing more than that.

But Hugh seemed to have no intention of keeping their embrace chaste and pure. He wanted more, and so did Jemima.

She could feel his heat, feel the longing in his arms now that they were both wrapped around her. There was a slight movement, and Jemima gasped as Hugh turned his head just enough to kiss her neck.

Jemima whimpered audibly as the rush of pleasure spread from that hot warm part of her neck where his kisses were falling, and it spurred him on. Hugh lavished his affection on her skin, hands tightly fixed on her waist, drawing her as close as possible. Jemima could feel her breasts starting to ache for his touch, and she closed her eyes, abandoning herself to the pleasure completely.

Pleasure that intensified when Hugh raised his head and transferred his lips' attention to her own.

Hugh teased her mouth open almost instantly, ravishing her mouth. He tasted of honey and strength, and Jemima could do nothing but raise her arms and entangle them in the jet-black hair that was as dark as the night around them.

Heady with emotion, Jemima was being swept away on a tide that was at once new to her and, at the same time, something that felt incredibly natural.

There was nothing like this, nothing like the soaring of passion with a man that felt so incredibly right as he held her in his arms. She wanted nothing more.

Hugh lifted his head, breaking the kiss for a moment, and Jemima tried to capture his lips once more. His breathing was ragged, and he smiled at her with longing.

"I want—" Jemima said breathlessly, her hands starting to move frantically, moving around to the front of his shirt and trying to quickly untie his cravat so she could once again see more of him, perhaps touch more of him. "I want—I don't know what I want, Hugh, but I want you."

It appeared that was not going to help Hugh control himself. He let out a deep groan, and in an instant, he had lowered his hands to her bottom, lifted her up, and placed her on the balcony railing.

"I know what you want," he said in a fervent tone, standing before her and cradling her head in his hands, "and I will never make you do anything that you do not want to, you hear me, Jemima?"

She nodded, unable to speak, unable to understand exactly what he meant but hoping that it was exactly what she suspected.

Hugh seemed to hesitate, seemed to think for a moment

whether or not what he was about to do was appropriate—but Jemima reached out a hand and pulled his jacket close to her.

She kissed him, her tongue venturing timidly at first into his mouth, and then boldly as she felt him melt into her and moan.

His hands moved down from her mouth and onto her knees, startling her slightly but not breaking their kiss. Jemima could feel her knees moving slightly apart, as one of Hugh's hands moved to her neck and caressed it to the point where Jemima could not focus any longer.

Now her legs were open, Hugh moved closer to her, standing within her knees, and Jemima instinctively wrapped her legs around him.

"Jemima," he moaned darkly, "you have no idea what you are doing to me."

But Jemima knew. She could feel the strong hard length of him, now they were so close, feel how the power of their ardor had a physical effect on him.

She laughed quietly. "I think it is you driving me wild, Hugh—I want more of you, I must have more."

At her words, he cast reserve to the wind, and Jemima gasped. One of his hands was on her breast, and she could feel every inch of his warmth. His thumb had found her nipple, budding through the thin silk, and he gently teased it back and forth, causing shooting sparks to fly through her body. His other hand had pushed up her long skirt and was stroking the softness of her thigh, making her quiver all over.

All this while his mouth had captured her lips once again, and Hugh was kissing her as if she was his last hope on the planet, as if letting her go would mean losing his own life.

Jemima was almost overcome. She could feel her center growing warm, and there was a wetness in that secret place that was starting to ache. Shivers of pleasure and bliss were rocketing round her, and it was all she could do to maintain her balance on the railing.

Hugh was seemingly suffering from the same feelings, as he

EMILY E K MURDOCH

moaned in her mouth each time his fingers brushed up against the soft curls that hid her secret place. Jemima gasped, almost a scream, as his fingertips brushed against her. His hands, so gentle and yet so strong, were drawing feelings out of her body she never thought could be possible.

"Hugh," Jemima moaned in the short break between kisses, "I want you to know—I need you to that...I have never...this is all new to me, and I haven't—before..."

"I know," he said simply, "and I cannot believe that you are trusting me with you."

Jemima arched her back as his finger and thumb pinched around her nipple and twisted a shock of pleasure through her core.

"Oh, God, Jemima," Hugh whispered, and his lips burned into hers once again.

Her hands moved to the buttons on his jacket, and although she wondered how on earth she was going to be able to concentrate long enough to remove them, her subconscious knew what she wanted and seemingly was happy to oblige. Before a moment had passed, the buttons were undone, and the jacket was dropped to their feet.

Jemima moved her hands to his chest, exploring the feeling of the strength and power that was under the linen shirt. Hugh quivered with every touch, whimpering slightly as he kissed her, as his hardness flexed, pushing itself toward her.

"Jemima," he murmured, his fingers stroking her to a rhythm now as she arched against his touch, desperate for more.

And then, suddenly, she was blind, pleasure rocketing through her. Jemima could barely see as Hugh's fingers brought her to such a crest of pleasure, she cried out his name, a cry stifled by his lips as he brought her gently back down to earth.

Hugh lifted his head from hers. "Jemima, I—"

"Jemima? Jemima where are you?"

Protected by the darkness of the night, Hugh acted quickly. A quick removal of his hand from her secret place joined with his second hand to lift Jemima back onto the ground.

Jemima could hardly think, hardly keep herself balanced. What had just occurred? Her legs quivered, pleasure still rippling out from her body.

What had Hugh done? What had they just shared, beyond the most utter pleasure a person could know?

"Jemima?"

"Ready to face the world?" Hugh whispered as Jemima tried to establish whether her hair was respectable enough to be seen. Would anyone guess? Would they know, merely by looking at her, that she had shared something so precious yet so scandalous, she was now a wanton woman?

Jemima shook her head slightly. "I would rather have carried on with you."

Hugh groaned with passion in his voice. "If we are not very careful, we shall end up doing something that we regret."

Jemima's eyes widened, but she did not pretend to misunderstand his meaning. "I would not have regretted a thing," she said simply.

She swallowed as she looked up at him. "It's all I can manage to prevent myself from asking you to sweep me back into your arms and lay me on the balcony."

Hugh groaned as he picked up his crimson jacket. "You are killing me, Jemima."

"Jemima?" Arabella's voice was worried now.

Jemima sighed. "I am here, Arabella."

She knelt down and lifted Hugh's crutch, handing it to him without a word before walking back into the ballroom.

CHAPTER NINE

"A ND HE'S REALLY gone?" Selina's eyes were wide and disbelieving. "Truly?"

Arthur gave a heavy sigh. "Yes."

Jemima had been expecting the news to be confirmed, but it was still a shock to hear at the breakfast table.

She sat beside her father at the head of the table, with Caroline beside her and the baby of the family, Sophia, on the other side. There were yawns from all quarters.

The family had overslept that morning, so their usual breakfast at nine o'clock had been postponed until eleven o'clock. Exhaustion and nerves filled the room, but Jemima was quiet for different reasons.

Last night. She could still hardly believe it.

"Jemima, you have no idea what you are doing to me."

Him? She was the one who had experienced something so unbelievable, so shocking, so wild, that her body had still not quite recovered.

And she wanted it again. Her body was greedy for that sort of pleasure. She wanted to take it again, her body arching with pleasure, and she wanted to give it, somehow, to Hugh. She wanted to see his eyes widen, to hear him cry out her name.

She was finding it difficult to get last night's encounter with Captain Hugh Rotherham out of her mind. Sometimes she thought she had dreamt it, but it was so clear in her memory.

It had certainly not felt like a dream, except in its most fantastical parts. That a man like Hugh should be interested in her! That such things could be done, and with just a few fingers...

"And Stuart—Dr. Walsingham, that is, is in complete shock," said Caroline quietly. She was much more reserved than usual, and Jemima could see that her eyes were heavy.

Caroline, it appeared, had cried through most of the night. Instead of the usual cream-colored gowns she preferred, she had taken out her mourning wear and was dressed in her only black gown.

Sophia asked quietly, "What does that mean for you, Caroline?"

Caroline frowned as she started to speak. "It is complicated...the family tree is a complex one, and I am not entirely sure... I think there is little change, but Walsingham said...I do not think we should speak of the dead."

"Come now, darling," said Selina, a hand to her forehead. "There must be more to it than that."

Jemima noted with interest that for once, Caroline did not seem interested in discussing her Dr. Walsingham. But she had another interest, too, and decided to take advantage of the fact she was seated by her father.

"Papa," she said quietly, "I wish to know your opinion on Captain Rotherham."

Arthur swallowed his mouthful, and after wiping his mouth with his handkerchief, asked casually, "Was he unwell when he arrived?"

Jemima was confused. She played with her fork, not heeding the conversation around her. "No, Captain Rotherham was perfectly well when I last saw—"

"Not that we knew of," Selina answered, and Jemima sighed. Of course, that question had not been for her. "But then, Dr. Walsingham had not seen his extended family for several years, he told me once at a card party."

"And he has no other family?"

Caroline shook her head, hardly listening it seemed.

"...do not you think, Caroline?"

Jemima looked up when she realized Caroline had not answered her mother's question. Her sister was staring at her plate, moving a half-eaten warm roll around with her fingers.

"I said," repeated her mother, "I am sure Dr. Walsingham will be very busy now, organizing his great-uncle's will now he is the only living family, do not you think, Caroline?"

Eyes around the table flickered over to Caroline, who would still not meet anyone's gaze.

"I have no wish to speak of this," she said finally in a quiet voice.

"Papa," Jemima said urgently in a low tone to her father, "I must speak with you."

"Hmm?" Arthur turned to her absentmindedly. "What exactly about, my child?"

"About Captain Rotherham. I wondered—"

"Not this again, Jemima—we have said it, if we have said it a thousand times, you are not in Parliament, and so you have no control over the military decisions of this country, and no, we do not want to hear your thoughts of what you would do if you were! Ah, the post!" Arthur looked pleased as a footman entered with a series of envelopes on a silver tray.

Sophia swallowed a large mouthful and shouted, "Anything for me, Papa? I'm expecting a letter from Cousin Maria."

"I'm hoping for a note from Joy and Harmony," Arabella called across her sister. "I was hoping that I would have received a letter from Esther or Lucy by now, but I suppose it is too much to expect from them, they always forget to attend to their manners. Is it there, Papa?"

Jemima sighed and focused on her breakfast once more as the footman brought the silver tray to their father. Picking the letters off the tray, Arthur Fitzroy looked through them with an interested eye.

"Another letter from the bank, ridiculous fools—I shall have to go back there tomorrow, Selina, my love, this is getting quite preposterous—and something that looks to me to be in a solicitor's hand...yes, that is for me, as well. Ah, here we have a letter for you, Sophia, I hope Maria and her family are well...and what is this? A letter for Jemima?"

Jemima's head snapped up.

In her father's hand was a small piece of parchment folded over and over many times. It had been sealed with red wax, and as her father turned it around in his fingers, she could see a large, neat hand had written her name on the front.

Miss Jemima Fitzroy

"A letter for Jemima?" Arabella, seated opposite her, accidentally let a large dob of preserve fall from her roll. "From whom?"

"I cannot tell," mused her papa. "I certainly do not recognize the hand."

Jemima smiled weakly. "I am sure if I was given leave to open it, I could answer all your questions!"

Sophia laughed, but Arabella's serious face did not shift.

"I was not aware that you were in correspondence with anyone," she said gravely. "Is it Joy? Or Audrey—I know you last saw her at her wedding, perhaps it is a note from her."

Jemima had no reason to suspect the note had been sent to her by Hugh, no way at all for her to tell from the handwriting if it were he who had penned it.

Yet who else could possibly be writing to her?

She could not take her eyes from it as her father turned it over and over in his hands. "I think I should perhaps open it, you know," he said finally in a deliberate voice.

Gasps were heard up and down the table, but Jemima was only aware of her own voice. "Papa, please! I am one and twenty years old, I am no child who needs protecting!"

"But you are my daughter," he reminded her with a serious

look on his face, "and under my protection. Who knows what salacious gossip this letter may contain?"

Jemima could feel her heart thumping painfully against her chest. On the mere chance it could possibly be from Hugh, it was imperative she was able to open it alone, with the eyes of no one on either it or her. To think her father could be the first to gaze upon the page on which Hugh had written...

"Really, Arthur," cut in Selina in a calm but forceful tone, "Jemima is quite right. She is not a babe in arms any longer, and I see no harm from a mere letter."

For the first time that Jemima could remember, she shot a grateful look down the table at her stepmother. Selina returned her look with a bemused smile, then looked down at the apple sitting on her plate, waiting to be eaten.

"Hmm." Arthur did not sound convinced, but after a few more seconds of deliberation, he offered Jemima her letter.

She tried not to sound too pompous when she said, "*Thank you*, Papa."

It was somewhat difficult, and what was even worse was that after such a fuss, all eyes in the room were now on her.

"Are you not going to open it?" Sophia asked, curiously.

Arabella nodded. "After such a long wait to gain ownership of it, are you not wild to see what it says?"

Jemima smiled. "Not yet. Not here, at any rate."

"Well, I've got other things to attend to," said Caroline quietly.

"And I'll come with you," said her mother. "After all, you cannot be expected to plan an entire wedding by yourself, can you?"

Soon, the only two left were Jemima and her father.

"I was up this early and realized we had not spoken properly in a while, Jemima," said her father genially. "I often find that the earlier I awake in the morning, the more that I achieve in the day. I would not wish to be slovenly and then complain I never had time for anything, like young Sophia."

Jemima smiled. It was not her wish to avoid her father—far from it, it was almost a miracle she had him alone—but at the same time, she had no wish to lie to him. A falsehood was the only response to questions pertaining to her plans for that day, and she would be obliged to give it if he asked.

"So," her father said happily, "where have you been off to, Jemima my dear? Do not think it has gone unnoticed, your scurrying about here and there—or I should say there and there, as here is not a place you seem to be frequenting in these last weeks."

Although she knew eventually the question would come, Jemima hesitated. She had not considered the reply she was to give. How could she even attempt to explain her walks with Hugh, her conversations with him, her understanding of him in new and exciting ways...

"Well?"

Jemima swallowed. Her weeks had been so taken up with Captain Hugh Rotherham there was little else she could say. Though they had not spoken of it, there seemed to be a mutual understanding that they would keep their affections a secret.

But their secret was no secret at all.

"Jemima Fitzroy," her father said sternly, placing his knife and fork down on the table, and staring at her seriously. "You have a gentleman friend you have neglected to inform me about."

Jemima sighed. "Perhaps, Papa."

"Perhaps?"

"Well," said Jemima, fiddling with the cutlery by her plate. "I am not sure if you are aware, Papa, but in the last five years I have hardly been inundated with offers from young men."

"Or old men," said Arthur, who had bequeathed his dry and sarcastic humor to his eldest child.

Jemima glared. "Your rude comments are noted, and unappreciated."

Her father could not help but smile. "Child," he said gently, "I think you are fully aware of the reasons why your friends have been taken up the aisle ahead of you. I think your character demanded someone greater than the idiots you constantly met with in the Assembly Rooms, at dinners, and at card parties."

"Papa!" Jemima's anger finally escaped its confines. "Your close watch on me has been a humiliation for so long, do you have to be so difficult about a conversation of a man who actually cares for me?"

"Humiliate you?" Her papa looked aghast. "It was never my intention to become a device for mortification! Embarrassment was not a factor I considered present in my protection of you."

His last words hung in the air.

Jemima, ever aware that at any moment a sister could descend the stairs and discover them, spoke quickly. "Protection?"

Arthur smiled weakly. "My darling girl," he said gently. "Do you really think I stand around to inspect you, make silence critiques of your appearance, note your mistakes in dancing, and silently comment on your lack of ability to keep a gentleman's attention during a conversation?"

Jemima blushed. In truth, she had done.

"Do you remember Mr. Jettle?"

Blinking at the change in conversation, she nodded. "He was that young man who we met at the card party General Hillsborough laid on last summer. I did not like him and could not place my finger on the reason."

"And you are an excellent judge of character," smiled her father. "Yet, I am not so. It has always been my wish you would choose a young man of great character, but I was...concerned I would not recognize him when you did. And so, I became a student."

"A...a student?"

"I followed your instinct, and discovered young Mr. Jettle had substantial gambling debts in Brighton." Her father smiled. "And do you remember Mr. Browning?"

Jemima could do nothing but nod.

"You turned up your nose at him as soon as he laughed at

something you said about the war effort costing our country too much. He was caught smuggling brandy a month later, did you not hear?"

Jemima swallowed. "And so, you have watched out for...for all the fools who were uninterested in me, and I had no desire to know better?" Jemima's words were full of wonder, her eyes unbidden filling with tears. "And all of this time, I suffered under the belief that you were noting my own errors."

"Errors?" Her father blinked and took his daughter's chin in his hand. "I do not think you have made an error, certainly when it comes to gentlemen since you first came out into Society—and I do not say that lightly."

Jemima stared at her father in amazement. "You know, Papa, I think there is still much that I have to learn about you."

Arthur laughed kindly. "My dear, I think you will have little time to do it as Mrs. Rotherham."

"Rotherham," Jemima whispered. "Rotherham—Captain Rotherham. You think he cares for me? Truly?"

Her father nodded, a sad sort of smile on his face. "Captain Hugh Rotherham. Commended in dispatches for his bravery in France, from a good family with a good stable income, well-respected in both my club and his own, and...and I suspect, the owner of my daughter's heart."

Jemima's mouth fell open.

"Now child, you forget yourself," her father said quietly. "You are so like your mother. I wish that you could have known her. The older I see you grow, the easier I find it to understand you, for you explain yourself just like her, every feeling that passes through your heart displayed on your face in an instant. When she...when she died, I was inconsolable. I think I clung to you as though you could keep me afloat in a strange world, now it did not contain my beloved wife."

She had never heard her Papa speak of her mother in this way. "I did not know that," she said softly. "We never seem to talk about her."

Her papa sighed. "She was a marvelous woman, and I feel the lack of her, even now, even with your stepmother. Selina is an admirable mother to her children, but I fear you lack the warmth of your own mother's comfort."

Refusing to cry was the only way to conduct this conversation, Jemima reminded herself. She would not cry.

"I am glad I spoke of her with you," said Arthur gently, placing his hand on hers. "We should do it more often."

"Do what more often?"

Jemima and her father twisted their heads suddenly to see where the new voice had come from and saw Sophia standing in the doorway.

"Are you off for the day, child?" Arthur stood and went to embrace his youngest daughter, and the moment between him and Jemima was broken.

But Jemima thought more contentedly than she had done in a long time, it had happened. And it could happen again. As she took a sip of tea, she tried to find balance once more in her soul. Her papa did trust her; he was merely attempting to understand her. He considered Hugh a good match.

Mrs. Rotherham.

"Oh, and Jemima?"

Jemima looked up and saw that the rest of the family had entered the room again. The morning conversation had moved swiftly on to the matter of Stuart's great-uncle—there seemed to be some sort of legal problem; Jemima had not been paying attention—but now her father called her name.

Jemima rested her cup of tea back onto the saucer. "Yes, Papa?"

Her father's eyes twinkled. "Do not forget to invite your friend to dinner tonight, will you? I am anxious to meet them. I am sure that we all are."

He cast a look at his wife who immediately said, "Yes, Jemima, we long to meet your friend. Do invite her for tonight, I shall easily be able to ask Mrs. Castle to lay on an extra setting at the table."

Jemima caught her Papa's eye and tried not to laugh. Her stepmother's assumption that her friend would be wearing skirts and not breeches was not lost on either of them.

"Are you sure, Mama?" Jemima said respectfully. "It will be very near Christmas, after all. I would not want my friend to be an imposition."

Selina waved her hand with a smile. "No imposition whatsoever."

Suddenly Caroline burst out, "But what is to be done?"

Jemima looked wildly around the room, but it seemed as though everyone else had followed this perfectly. That showed her, she thought, for not paying attention this morning.

And the letter her father had given her was still in her hand. Unopened.

"I will go and see my friend and invite them for tonight," she said quietly, quitting the table just as Caroline burst into tears.

It was unlike Caroline to cry, but Jemima had more pressing matters on her mind. She must find Hugh immediately. She must find him and tell him that...what to tell him? To all intents and purposes, they had received her father's blessing, and surely that meant...

"Did you ever open that letter?"

Arabella's question was innocently meant, but Jemima was in no mood to share the contents of anything personal that morning.

"No," replied Jemima. "Not yet. And even when I have, I shall not be sharing its contents!"

With those words, and ignoring the disappointment from her family, she exited the room.

She saw with gladness that no one had followed her. The letter felt small in her hand, yet weighty with its potential import, and after gathering a large woolen shawl around her shoulders, she let herself out into the garden.

The air was cold, but the sun was battling on, attempting to shine as best it could against the December wind. Jemima shivered slightly but persevered. With five sisters, any time and space one could find for oneself ought to be treasured gladly.

Jemima had only one place in her mind that would be suitable for opening her letter. Stepping lightly, she walked up the steps to the garden terrace and leaned against the balcony. In the coolness of the day, if she closed her eyes, she could almost pretend that she was with Hugh, imagining his arms around her once more.

But now was not the time to imagine. If she was correct, there was his handwriting already clutched in her hand.

Her fingers were starting to become numb, so she concentrated on the matter at hand and gazed down at her name written in an unfamiliar hand.

"Could this be Hugh's handwriting?" she whispered to herself. "Could he have written this to me?"

There was only one way to discover the truth.

Jemima pulled the letter apart and found to her disappointment there were only a few short lines inside—but as she read them, her heart began to flutter, and the smile which had disappeared from her lips appeared again.

Jemima,

I am desperate to meet with you, and hope you share my desire to speak more about our acquaintance...friendship...I know not what to call it.

I beg you to meet me, I implore you. You will see me at our bench at noon, where I will ever be,

your Hugh

"Your Hugh," she said in a soft voice. "Your Hugh."

No matter how many times she read those words, or whispered them in an undertone, they did not yield up their secrets.

If he was her Hugh, did that make her his Jemima? What did he mean by this—and what would he have to say to her at noon?

The thought of noon struck her forcefully. It had been five past the hour of eleven when they had sat down to breakfast together, and it was at least an hour after that. Rushing inside, Jemima glanced at the nearest clock and saw with a groan that the hands told her it was a quarter past noon already.

She was late. He was waiting for her—he may even believe she had decided not to arrive.

There was no time to change, no time to alter her appearance in any way. Jemima did not even exchange the woolen shawl from her shoulders for her much warmer pelisse.

Nothing could distract her. She must make it to Hyde Park.

But I am already late, she thought desperately, throwing shut the front door as she ran down the stairs to the street. *How long will Hugh wait there for me: five minutes, maybe ten?*

The Christmas bustle of London had not abated in the slightest, and there were times when Jemima considered calling a carriage to get her there more speedily.

She did not notice the rain at first, busy as she was with navigating through the London crowds. But after a few minutes, the woolen shawl around her shoulders started to grow heavy, and she could no longer ignore the wet hair starting to stick to her face.

If finding a hansom was difficult minutes before, it was impossible now. She was only a minute or two away. She was going to make it.

Jemima turned a corner and began to pray silently that if Hugh was leaving Hyde Park, he would leave by the same gate that she was entering so that she could catch him.

He must not be permitted to leave without her.

She was sure to see him. The park was almost empty, the vast majority of people leaving to escape the rain falling heavier now, though the warmth of the day was unusual, and the rain easily forgotten when seeking out one's love.

Jemima started to run, unladylike as it was, desperate to ensure he did not leave without telling her...telling her whatever it was he had to say to her.

Running fast, breathing deeply, barely paying any attention to her surroundings as she went, Jemima was unfortunate enough to crash straight into someone as she turned a corner on the path.

Down she tumbled onto the wet grass, entangled with the gentleman who had been unlucky enough to be in her way.

Jemima did not heed him, hastily trying to scramble onto her feet to continue on to the park where Hugh and she had first talked, first connected, first started to learn about each other.

The gentleman she had brought to the ground said angrily, "In the name of God, what's the hurry?"

Jemima froze, her attempt to untangle her legs from the stranger halting. Because he was no stranger.

It was Captain Hugh Rotherham.

Unable to help herself, Jemima began to laugh. She gave up her futile attempts to right herself and laughed at the absurdity of it all.

"Jemima?" Hugh's face was a picture—splattered with mud once again, and a dazed expression on his features. "Jemima, is that really you, or have I knocked my head in the fall?"

Jemima snorted with laughter and put a hand to her face as the giggles poured out of her. The rain continued to fall heavily, and she could see now that they were completely alone in the park. There was no one around them for miles, and they pulled themselves up to a sitting position, facing each other.

Hugh's face tried to stay stern, but he eventually gave way to a smile. "I cannot believe that, of all the people exiting this park, I am the one that you bring to the ground."

"I do apologize," Jemima said, her laughter abating but her smile remaining. "Although it does seem to be rather a pattern, don't you think?"

Hugh nodded wryly. "Too much of a pattern if you ask me. I have a crutch for a reason, you know."

"I am so glad I found you. I was worried you would have returned home, that you would not wait for me."

"I did wait for you," Hugh countered. "And where would I go? I have no home, merely billets I share with three other officers—three men currently rehearsing their drumming as we speak! And," he said with a hint of steel in his voice, "I think it is ridiculous we are having this conversation whilst sitting on wet grass in the middle of a rain cloud."

"Oh, I don't know," said Jemima. "I suppose we cannot get any wetter than we already are, so we may as well stay put. We shall not receive much shelter from the trees this close to Christmas."

Hugh's smile disappeared. A worried look shadowed his face to be replaced with a sad one.

"Miss Fitzroy," he began, but he was immediately over-ruled.

"Miss Fitzroy?" Jemima said, frowning. "Hugh, I thought...I thought after what we had shared, we were beyond that."

"We were," replied Hugh sadly, "yet I must ask that you call me Captain Rotherham from now on, and I shall endeavor to call you Miss Fitzroy. It will be easier that way."

Jemima could not understand him; it was as though there was a part of the conversation that she had missed. After all their conversations, all their debates, after the kisses she had taken from him, that he had given willingly, after last night on the balcony, when he had given her such pleasure...

"Hugh—Captain Rotherham, I mean," she said quietly. "I do not understand. Have I...have I done something to offend you?"

It was the only possible explanation she could see for why his gaze would not quite meet hers.

Hugh hastily said, "No!"

"Then you wish to end our friendship for no reason other than the fact that I was late for our meeting!" said Jemima dramatically. It was only when Hugh bit his lip that her heart sank. "I...I was only joking, Hugh—Captain. I do not wish to end our acquaintance at all, and I did not think you did. But I can see in your face...you no longer wish to know me."

She could not help the pain in her voice, echoing the agony in her heart. After all, she had shared with him, after the innocence she had given him—he could just walk away?

"It is not as simple as that," bit back Hugh. Jemima blanched at the anger in his voice, causing him to sigh heavily. "Miss Fitzroy, I will be as honest with you as you are always so honest with everyone that is around you, and I beg that you will forgive me the impertinence."

Jemima nodded. Her hair was soaking wet now, and she could see that his was as well. The jet-black hair clung to his face, his jawline even more distinct with the raindrops falling from it. She had barely noticed that her green cotton dress was sopping wet, hugging her figure as the rain continued to pour down.

Hugh swallowed. "Miss Fitzroy, you are unlike anyone I have ever met. The friendship you have accorded me and the passion I find are...are extraordinary. Nothing compares to them, and the thought of not having you in my acquaintance, let alone my life, is more abhorrent to me than life itself."

Jemima tried to calm her breathing, but it did not seem possible. All she could do was stare into Hugh's eyes and try not to drown.

"What are you saying?" she breathed.

"I admit it," he said helplessly. "I am falling in love with you."

Jemima's heart leapt. "Then—"

"No," he said forcefully, stopping her from speaking. "I have no wish for you to compromise yourself by promising emotions I should not be permitted to feel!"

Swallowing, Jemima repeated quietly, "Should not be permitted to feel?"

Hugh shook his head. "I love you, Jemima Fitzroy, more than any soul on this world. Yet, I cannot marry you."

CHAPTER TEN

J EMIMA SAT THERE, aghast.

"You love me? How is that possible?" The rational, more cynical part of her shouted loudly in her mind that they had only known each other a few weeks.

And yet…

Yet was that not typical for many who met their spouses in the Season? A recommendation from a mutual acquaintance, a few dances, a dinner with each other's parents…and that was it.

A marriage betrothal could occur.

Had she and Hugh not shared far more than that? *More*, Jemima thought with a flush, *than some wedded couples shared*?

Their hopes, their passions, their debates. Their moment on the balcony.

Was that not more than some wives ever gained?

No, this was ridiculous, Jemima tried to tell herself. In love, with Hugh Rotherham, a man she did not know existed two months ago?

The more emotional side of her, a side she rarely allowed to take control but was always whispering in the background murmured: *and?*

An hour's acquaintance was enough for her to decide against many of the young men thrown in her path. Why then were several weeks not sufficient for her to decide in favor of Captain

Hugh Rotherham?

It took her several swallows to remove the dryness from her mouth, before she was ready to speak again, and it was with difficulty. "You…"

Hugh was not waiting for her to speak; he had already pushed himself up to his feet, retrieved his crutch, and looked at her with sad eyes.

"You really believe you can just walk away, without a look back at me?"

Hugh was already walking toward the exit for the park, toward his lodgings, but Jemima was easily able to keep up with him. Pushing herself to her feet, she reached his side within a moment, fighting the urge to take his hand in hers.

If only she could make him see…

"You honestly think leaving me here soaking wet in the park is an option for you?" Jemima spluttered. "You say you love me, yet in the same breath proclaim you have no wish to marry me?"

"Jemima, what can I offer you?" Hugh said sadly, not looking at her as they left the park and started down the street. "I have no prospects, and we are at war! When it is over, I will have no occupation to protect you and keep you happy in the situation you are currently accustomed to."

"But—" Jemima was unsure what she was going to say, but she was interrupted before she could think.

"What of your ideals?" Hugh spoke roughly, and some of his words were drowned out as they stepped inside a building, which Jemima assumed was his billets. She did not think. She merely followed him, unwilling to allow this conversation to end. "Change the way you are, that is the last thing that I would want!"

With a sudden lurch, Jemima realized they were climbing the stairs that would lead straight to his—to Captain Hugh Rotherham's rooms. And they were empty.

Door flung wide open, Hugh strode forth as best he could, and Jemima hurriedly closed the door behind her. The last thing she wanted when Captain Hugh Rotherham ended their acquaintance forever was for spectators to listen in.

"Your thoughts and opinions make you who you are," Hugh was saying, "and that is the woman I fell in love with! Changing you would be akin to murdering the old Jemima to allow a new Jemima, one that I do not know, to be born instead!"

"That is the biggest pile of nonsense I have ever heard in my life! Do you really think so little of me that you believe me unchanging, unwilling to ever grow, to learn, to change my mind?"

Hugh paused from his uncomfortable pacing to stare at Jemima. "Change—change your mind?"

"I do not say I have completely changed every opinion," she said quickly. "I cannot pretend to love war, and I still think we do almost nothing for our veterans who return home—but knowing you, appreciating exactly what it is like to go off to war, with friends as close as brothers by your side, to do what must be done…do you think that I am of marble, that I would not be moved by such knowledge?"

"So you are willing, are you, to become a soldier's wife?" shot back Hugh. "To become a soldier's widow? Because we're going back to France, Jemima, I received the news today, and, by God, do you think I could leave you here if you were my wife?"

"Wife?"

Jemima stared almost unblinking as the word echoed between them.

Wife. Hugh's wife.

Hugh almost looked amazed that he had said it. As though it had been teasing around the edges of his mind but had not expected it to slip out.

"It is not that I do not wish to marry you," said Hugh slowly, his dark eyes flashing. "It is that I must not."

The rain was still falling outside of the paned windows, and the two of them were still soaking wet from their stroll in the park.

Jemima thought she would be cold, but she wasn't. Not in the presence of Hugh. Not as they spoke of such incendiary things.

She looked at him with eyes full of confusion. "Hugh—Captain Rotherham—are you in earnest? Are you truly saying that because you are a captain in the army and you march to the drums of war, you do not wish to be with me?"

"I love you," burst out Hugh, his face determined, "yet what could I possibly say to your father when I asked for your hand? That I am the son of Harold Rotherham, accountant, with little certainty to speak of and no prospects?"

Jemima shook her head. "You cannot comprehend your worth and value, can you?"

Hugh broke off his gaze and picked at the grass stuck to his coat.

"You see the crutch that lies before you," he said quietly. "It does not take a genius to suggest that a worse fate may be waiting for me in France, and then what should I do? I could return to you blind, or deaf, or without a limb altogether."

"Or you may not come back at all."

These words caused Hugh to look up abruptly.

"You are shocked?" Jemima asked wryly. "Yet you talk of such things willingly, without consideration of my fears or countenance? Captain Hugh Rotherham," her voice turning serious, "you are a man who does not know how fortunate he is, how truly excellent is your character. Why, I have known you just above a month, and I am standing here soaking wet in an attempt to convince you of a worth so much more than the meager value you assign yourself!"

"I have nothing to offer you," Hugh said in a dark persistent tone, "and—"

"No," interrupted Jemima forcefully. "I do not care if you are determined to repeat your nonsense over and over again until this rain stops, the sun goes down, or the world ends. You cannot convince me that you are without merit and without worth."

She could not understand from where the words came, but

she had to speak them. She had to pour out her heart, had to ensure he knew, that Hugh knew just how wonderful he was.

Even if he did not marry her. Even if he followed the drums of war with no promises to her whatsoever.

"Your kindness to me, your bravery, your goodness of heart, far more wide-reaching than my own—and your passion," and here Jemima colored slightly, but her voice did not hesitate, "your passion for life as well as for myself! All of these add up to a man who is worth something even more precious than anything I can ever give you."

During her speech, her hands had somehow managed to become entangled with his own. The space between them had been covered, though she was unsure who had stepped toward the other, or if they had both moved to close the gap.

They had to be closer together. They were drawn together, inexorably.

His hands were strong, and Jemima grasped them, not taking her eyes away from those of Hugh as an internal battle occurred within them. At once calm, and at the same time wild with emotion and thought, Hugh stayed motionless and quiet.

But Hugh seemed to know her better than she knew herself. "Do not suppose, my love, that I am unaware of your multitude of merits," he said with a smile.

Jemima laughed awkwardly and looked away. "I am well aware of my own failings, do not fear. There is a reason, as my father would put it, that I have survived these last five Seasons without eliciting any sort of courtship or offer of marriage. I am rude, abrupt, and unfaltering when speaking, with little regard for Society's desire to keep this polite, quiet, and—"

"Perfection," cut in Hugh, his smile deepening. "Why do you think I have been so drawn to you, Jemima, from the very first moment we met? Why do you think I have sought out your company, accepted your father's ridiculous invitation for me to prance around and make an idiot of myself?"

"Politeness is an art form," Jemima said with a sardonic smile, her hands still captive to Hugh's, "and just because you have perfected it does not mean—"

"You are the one for me, Jemima." Hugh's voice was completely serious, and Jemima blinked away what she was sure were rain drops dripping from her hair. It could not possibly be tears. "No one else. You and I walk to the same drumbeat. You are intelligent and witty and beautiful and incredibly caring. You outweigh my value, were they to be measured."

Jemima smiled. "You have more to offer me," she said, her hands squeezing Hugh's, "than any other man I have ever met."

She waited once more for his reaction to her words, but he seemed to be stunned, gazing at her with an expression of confusion. Eventually, she remarked quietly, "And what do you have to say to that, Hugh Rotherham?"

The sound of his name seemed to release all the passion and tension within him.

Hugh groaned and, loosening his hands from her own, he reached to cup her face as he fiercely took possession of her lips.

Jemima sighed into the kiss, the pleasure of his tongue ravishing the soft warmness of her mouth. The forcefulness of his ardor was welcome as he possessed her like no other. There had never been anyone like Hugh, no one at all, and she wanted no other.

When he broke away from their kiss to stare into her eyes, she said breathlessly, "There is no other man for me than you, Hugh Rotherham."

"Jemima," Hugh groaned into her mouth, releasing her face and, instead, using his hands to draw her body closer to him.

Jemima was barely aware that they were seated on the bed in Hugh's room, grateful there was no one to see the disgraceful display that she and Hugh were portraying. Her skin was damp, her dress clinging to every inch of it. Her nipples, desperate for Hugh's touch once again, had hardened, visible through her soaking wet gown, but she no longer felt any shame.

She was with Hugh. He loved her. Would marry her. He would be her husband.

He groaned once more, and deepening their kiss, his left arm moved around her waist keeping her tightly clasped to him, the other went in search of the softness of her breast.

Jemima knew they should be restrained, knew what they were enjoying was simply not done, especially alone and unwed—but why should she restrain herself when she was so willing, and they loved each other so much?

She gasped in his mouth when he found her peak, softly caressing the soft damp skin that could be accessed above her dress and then exploring down to the ripe fullness of her breast. Her body was on fire, every inch of her desperate for the same attention.

Her hands fumbled with the buttons of his jacket, but she was better practiced now after the evening before on the garden balcony, and it took less than a thought for her to release him.

Hugh's shirt was so wet it was more of a window to his taut chest. Jemima opened her eyes in shock to see the strong muscles and the curls that rose up to his throat and delved down in a trail to the top of his trousers, her thoughts following them down as her fingers splayed across his chest.

"Hugh," she said in a ragged voice, "Hugh, I want—"

"I know," Hugh's voice was worse than her own, seemingly just able to construct words into a sentence. "I know what you want."

It took only a heartbeat, and Jemima was unsure exactly how he had done it, but suddenly she was facing the ceiling, her back on the soft dry sheets. Hugh looked down at her, his expression unreadable, as his breathing grew deeper and more hurried.

"Do you trust me?" Hugh said quietly. As the hardness between his legs met the softness of hers. Jemima tried not to think about the very thin and very damp two layers of clothing currently keeping them apart. "I do not wish to do anything that you are uncomfortable with, Jemima, my love."

Jemima stared into his eyes and raised a hand to pull him down even closer, his lips a mere breath away from hers.

"I would follow you anywhere," she said in a strong tone, "and I follow you now."

Hugh smiled, a smile Jemima had never seen before. All his concern seemed to melt away as water dripped from his torso, and he appeared to be entirely at peace.

But peace was not going to last, not when Hugh had permission to take her to the highest peaks of happiness he knew. Jemima hoped, as pleasure poured through her body and her mind became frayed and tangled, that he would give her that pleasure again. Surely, he knew what she wanted? Surely, he could see what she craved?

Propped up by his elbow, Hugh returned his lips to the place where they belonged: Jemima.

She opened her mouth willingly, taking him deeper into her, welcoming the sensations threatening to overwhelm her. As his lips massaged hers, his right hand moved to the ties at the top of her gown. Jemima whimpered into his mouth as she felt the tie pull and, eventually, fall open.

"You are so beautiful," Hugh whispered, breaking the kiss to look down at her. "So beautiful…"

It was fortunate, Jemima managed to think, that she had once again ignored her stepmother and only wore one petticoat today.

It was as damp as Hugh's shirt and just as transparent. His fingers brushed across her porcelain skin, still damp from the rain, and Jemima twitched, the mere touch enough to make her tremble.

In a moment, Hugh's hands had pulled down both gown and petticoat to her ankles, then looped them off them and tossed them to the floor.

Embarrassment should have coursed through Jemima's veins, and had it been any other man, she would have shied away, desperate to keep herself hidden.

But this was not any other man: this was Hugh.

Jemima arched her back slightly, unconsciously desperate for his touch to return to her.

"Oh, God, Jemima!"

It appeared Hugh could take no more. Lowering his head, he grazed the delicate skin just above her breasts with his lips. Jemima's short intake of breath was matched only by her desire to have him repeat the connection.

"More, more Hugh," she moaned.

He ventured lower, eventually reaching that ripe pink peak he had not yet tasted. Taking it into his mouth, he suckled, ensuring her other breast was not abandoned by bringing up his hand to fondle it delicately, and then more forcefully as their passion grew.

Jemima's eyes were wide as she gasped aloud. "Yes, yes!"

This was too much, too much pleasure surely that one person could experience. His teeth grazed her nipple, and she almost shouted out in desire. Where they were was forgotten, what was expected of them was forgotten—there was only this experience, this moment, this paradise.

Releasing her breasts, Hugh returned to her mouth, demanding her tongue with his own, worshipping her as his hands moved to her hips, adjusting their position so that they met with his.

It was impossible for Jemima to ignore the pooling of heat moving toward her secret place, and a dark longing was starting to build there.

She recognized it. It was the same desperation she had felt last night with Hugh's hardness between her thighs and his fingers stroking her secret place.

She did not understand it, but she welcomed it, all the same, giving herself entirely to Hugh and the incredible joy he drew from her.

Unbidden, untaught, Jemima drew one of her legs up and over Hugh, and he moaned in her mouth. The kiss became, if possible, more passionate, and Jemima reached for his shirt, desperately trying to pull it off, yearning for more contact than she was already given.

Madness, she thought wildly. It was madness coursing

through her veins, not blood—surely that could be the only reason why she was unable to contain the way she felt about Hugh every waking moment she was around him.

The fierceness of his face, the fiery stare he so frequently fixed upon her; there was no one his equal, no one she had ever encountered before who even started to compare.

Hugh broke their kiss and wrenched his shirt off over his head in one fluid motion.

"Are you ready for this?" he said, his voice jagged in the quiet of the room. "Because there is no going back from this, Jemima. Once you have experienced this, there is no going back."

"I have no wish to go back," she said, panting with desire. "I want you."

Hugh smiled, and the ache between her legs grew urgent.

"Now, Hugh," she said, reaching for him, "I want you now."

He needed no other invitation. Moving down once more above her, Hugh returned to satiate his appetite for her breasts, Jemima's eyes closing in uncontrolled pleasure.

But Hugh was doing so much more than that. Jemima was not consciously aware of it, too busy delighting in the adoration of his lips, but his hands moved slowly toward his breeches, unbuttoning them to release—

"Hugh," Jemima said weakly, "Hugh, what are you—oh!"

Her voice was suddenly cut off by the movement of his hand from the outside of her thigh to the inside. His hand rested there, her thigh quivering under the unexpected touch.

Jemima squirmed slightly, but Hugh kept his hand still, her movements not distracting enough to stop him from kissing her neck.

"Hugh…" Jemima moaned. She wanted more, so much more—she wanted what he had given her last night. She was already enjoying more sensuality than she could ever have dreamed of. Surely there could not be more intimacy than this?

Hugh's hand was no longer static; instead, it moved gently up her thigh until Jemima shouted out as unexpected jolts of pure lust sparked from the fingers that had lightly brushed over her curls.

"Oh, Hugh," she whimpered, arching her back so he could take in more of her breasts, trying to keep her bottom still so she did not interrupt whatever glorious thing he was doing with his hand.

"Hush," Hugh lifted his face so that he could look into her eyes, "I am about to take you somewhere you have never been before. Just lie back and enjoy this."

Jemima nodded, but it was difficult not to cry out as his fingers once more brushed the warm and sensitive skin in her secret place.

"Oh, God, Jemima, you are so wet." He dropped his head as if overcome.

Jemima did not have the breath to answer him. All she could do was lie back as instructed. His fingers circled around her heat, becoming wet from her, then soft strokes became harder, stronger, more rhythmic. Jemima twisted her hips as she felt herself starting to be carried away by something deep inside her, and Hugh smiled.

"I love you," he said, and then he spoke not one word more, dropping his mouth to her breasts.

Taking a nipple into his mouth, he tortured her. The combination of his mouth exploring her breast and returning to her mouth whenever her cries grew too great, and his hand moving steadily over and into her secret place...it was causing her whole body to be flooded with pleasure as she had never known.

It was too much surely—and yet with each passing moment the pleasure grew. She was nearing something, something akin to the peak she had felt yesterday, and though she was desperate to get there, she wanted to enjoy the journey just as much.

"Hugh," she moaned wildly, "Hugh, I love you!"

But he had no reply for her, unless she counted the sudden increase in speed. He seemed unable to stop himself, and Jemima was glad because the hot pooling feeling descending to her secret place was starting to make her vision darken.

Suddenly, she exploded. Parts of her body she had never been aware of before were on fire with pleasure and delight, and her secret place clenched unbidden around Hugh's hand. Her breasts tingled and sparked with desire, and Jemima had no choice but to cry out quietly in happiness.

Her muffled shouts subsided as the pleasure did, although even as Hugh raised his head, he continued to tenderly kiss her neck as the pleasure eased away.

Slowly, her body started to relax, and she opened her eyes to look up at Hugh.

"That," Jemima said shakily, "was…I do not think that I have the words for it."

Unbidden, she raised her lips for another kiss, and he obliged willingly.

They had kissed before, and Jemima was almost sure that they would spend the rest of their days kissing—yet this kiss was perfection. This was not the kiss of a man to a woman; this was a kiss from a husband to his wife. Her heart beat painfully, almost overpowering her.

Hugh smiled down at her, his love evident. "I know," he said quietly. He waited a moment, gazing down at her face, her breasts, her hips, her body which she revealed to him and no other. "And no matter what happens, wherever the drums of war may call me, your voice will always call over them louder, calling me home."

Jemima's eyes widened as Hugh shifted between her legs, and a spark of pleasure that was ever so memorable flushed through her body. Snow was starting to fall across the windowpanes now, not rain. It was going to be a white Christmas.

Hugh's smile widened, and a wicked look appeared on his face. "Ready to go again?"

About Emily E K Murdoch

If you love falling in love, then you've come to the right place.

I am a historian and writer and have a varied career to date: from examining medieval manuscripts to designing museum exhibitions, to working as a researcher for the BBC to working for the National Trust.

My books range from England 1050 to Texas 1848, and I can't wait for you to fall in love with my heroes and heroines!

Follow me on twitter and instagram @emilyekmurdoch, find me on facebook at facebook.com/theemilyekmurdoch, and read my blog at www.emilyekmurdoch.com.

Printed in the USA
CPSIA information can be obtained
at www.ICGtesting.com
LVHW020957231123
764770LV00027B/319